NO STRINGS

GOLDEN CROWN LITERARY AWARD WINNER

GERRI HILL

Bella
BOOKS

2009

Bella Books, Inc.
P.O. Box 10543
Tallahassee, FL 32302

Printed in the United States of America on acid-free paper
First Edition

Editor: Cindy Cresap
Cover Designer: Stephanie Solomon-Lopez

ISBN 10: 1-59493-147-x
ISBN 13: 978-1-59493-147-5

About the Author

Gerri Hill has thirteen published works, including 2007 GCLS winners *Behind the Pine Curtain* and *The Killing Room*, as well as GCLS finalist *Hunter's Way* and Lambda finalist *In the Name of the Father*. She began writing lesbian romance as a way to amuse herself while snowed in one winter in the mountains of Colorado, and hasn't looked back. Her first published work came in 2000 with *One Summer Night*. Hill's love of nature and of being outdoors usually makes its way into her stories, as her characters often find themselves in beautiful natural settings. When she isn't writing, Hill and her longtime partner, Diane, can be found at their home in East Texas, where their vegetable garden, orchard and five acres of woods keep them busy. They share their lives with two Australian shepherds, and an assortment of furry felines. For more, see her Web site: www.gerrihill.com.

DEDICATION

No Strings is dedicated to my pal Judy, the HP, and to all the other GGGs...WWWendy, Wingnut, Norma, WKS, Rubbin' Peg, Butch, JJ, Mo and Paula, Ann, Baby Raye, Babemm, Cheri, Adri, Ally, Sister Sara, Ana, Janet, JT, Mandy, Anneroo, Shannon, Dianne, Canadian Julie, Texas Julie, Shyfox, Lotuspeed...and the many others who found a family with the GGGs. Thank you.

ACKNOWLEDGMENT

Many thanks to my editor, Cindy Cresap. I have enjoyed working with you. And to Judy Underwood, thanks as always, for being a sounding board.

CHAPTER ONE

Morgan wiped the tears from her eyes again, thinking maybe she should have let Tina drive. The snow was coming down heavier now and she blinked several times, trying to clear her vision.

But all she could see was Jackson, his big trusting eyes watching her. *Oh, God.*

"You okay?"

Morgan shook her head. "No. I just can't believe he's gone."

"You kept him going as long as you could. You know that. The vet said it was well past time."

"And that's supposed to help? He's been my friend, my *partner* for eleven years. And now he's gone. Just like that." She wiped her face again as a tear slid down her cheek. Yes, just like that. She barely had time to realize what was happening. Within seconds of getting the shot, Jackson's eyes closed and it was almost as they say. *Putting him to sleep*. Almost. Because Jackson wasn't going to wake up. Not ever.

"I'm sorry, Morgan. I know he was your...your buddy. But you can get another puppy."

"No." Of that, Morgan was adamant. She would not go through this again. The heartache these last few months was nearly too much, knowing the end was near, knowing she'd be the one to make that decision, the decision to *put him to sleep*. "No. I can't get another dog."

"Give it some time."

"You think I'm being ridiculous, don't you?"

Tina shook her head. "Of course not. I've got two kids, and I often wondered if Jackson was treated better than my own children."

Morgan took a deep breath and tried to smile. "I guess getting him cremated was a good idea," she said. "I'd have a hell of a time trying to bury him in this mess."

"I think I'd rather brave the snow than try to dig a hole big enough for a ninety-pound Labrador in this mountain of rock."

"Yeah, okay. So that was a factor too," she said with a quiet laugh. Yeah. It was a factor. But for some reason, the thought of putting Jackson in a deep hole and covering him with dirt was less appealing than cremation. And Dr. Bryant said he'd find a nice decorative box to keep him in. No one would have to know that she kept him on her mantel, or on her dresser, or by the sofa. She rolled her eyes. Christ, she was turning into one of those old batty women and she wasn't even forty yet.

"It's snowing hard. I thought we were just supposed to get a dusting," Tina said.

"It's November and we haven't had a major storm yet. Maybe this is it."

"And you're taking it pretty well. You normally bitch for a week after our first storm."

"I hate being cold."

"You live in the Rocky Mountains. What do you expect?"

"I expect summertime temperatures in the seventies, that's

2

what I expect."

Tina laughed. "And you get that. You also get single digits in the winter and fifty feet of snow."

"You know, after my first winter here, I swore I would ask the Forest Service for a transfer. But after that first summer, I thought I was in heaven."

"Yeah. And winter follows summer."

"And it's been seven years. I'll do what I always do. Haul an ungodly amount of firewood to the house, take out my skis and lean them by the door and pretend I can't *wait* to get out in the snow."

"With all the cutbacks, you're not worried about them cutting your position?"

Morgan shook her head. "No. Charlie says I'm safe. Besides, that's why *you* get laid off every winter, so I can keep my job."

"I do not look at it as being laid off. I'm seasonal. And I vacation from October to April."

Morgan slowed as they topped the crest, looking down on Lake City, Colorado, below them. It was a beautiful sight. Everything clean and white, their first major snowfall of the season. Lake City survived only because of the tourists who flocked to the mountains during the summers, most to rent Jeeps and try their skill on the Alpine Loop. And with the lake and the clear trout streams, it was a fisherman's paradise. Most of the shops closed up after Labor Day though, making the town seem nearly deserted. The few that stayed open catered to the skiers who came to enjoy their pristine trails for a cross-country adventure, and the snowmobilers who enjoyed the numerous backcountry routes. The summer cabins closed too, and most of the resorts and bed-and-breakfasts, but the small lodge out by Slumgullion stayed open through winter, filling nearly all the rooms on weekends as snowmobilers headed right from the parking lot and onto the forest trails.

Even though she hated the cold, Morgan no longer thought about transferring to a warmer climate. Lake City had become home. The locals treated her as one of their own now and she knew everyone by name. Of course, that hadn't always been the case. She had been originally assigned to the Gunnison National Forest and Curecanti. She looked forward to working on Blue Mesa Lake. She'd been around water most of her life, coming from central Florida where lakes were more numerous than towns. But she hadn't been in Gunnison a day when they'd told her she'd been transferred. *Just down the road. Lake City. You'll love it.*

She remembered taking this very drive, seeing the same view, only in June. There was no huge lake she'd be patrolling, no medium-sized town that offered most modern conveniences. No, she was assigned to the Slumgullion Earthflow and Lake San Cristobal. She'd balked at first. With personnel limited, she'd be expected to wear a lot of hats, from game warden to campground host. Oh, sure, the San Juan Mountains were beautiful—spectacular, really—but after she'd spent two long, lonely summers in the remote Arizona desert, isolated from people and the world, she wasn't eager to embrace the remoteness of this tiny town. But after a week of Charlie dragging her all over the mountains, through Big Blue Wilderness, La Garita Wilderness, and up through the Umcompahgre National Forest, she was hooked. She'd even fallen in love with her tiny house, one of several the Forest Service owned. Tiny, yes, and close neighbors too, but that hardly mattered. She could walk out her back door and be swallowed up by the forest within ten feet. The four identical structures had been built nearly forty years ago to house the ever-changing personnel of the Forest Service. She and Jackson had made one of them into a home.

And now when she walked out her back door and into the forest, there wouldn't be an old yellow dog ambling beside her, too spent to even muster up the energy to chase the chipmunks that scurried ahead of them on the trail.

"Hey, have you heard anything about Charlie's daughter?" Tina asked.

Morgan frowned. "Other than he allegedly has one, no."

"I know. You've worked for the man seven years, you'd think

you'd have at least met her, right?"

"Or at least seen a picture."

"Well, Berta read an e-mail from her. Since he's retiring next year, apparently the daughter—"

"Wait. How did she read his e-mail? And *why* would she read his e-mail?"

"You know as well as I do that he barely knows what a computer is. She always opens his e-mail for him. And *why*... because she's nosy." Tina grabbed the dash as the truck slipped on the snow when Morgan turned onto their road. "Anyway, she's coming for a visit."

"The daughter?"

"Yeah. She's got a ski trip planned up to Crested Butte so she thought she'd pop over."

"I wonder if Charlie will bring her around." Morgan glanced quickly at Tina. "Why do you think he never talks about her? Or doesn't have any pictures or anything? It's almost like they're estranged."

"I guess not so much if she's coming to visit."

"Yeah, but it's just kinda strange. She's always been the phantom daughter." Morgan pulled to a stop in front of Tina's house. "Look, I appreciate you going with me." She turned to face her and gave a small smile. "I don't think I could have done it alone."

Tina leaned over and gave her a quick hug and kiss on the cheek. "We're best pals. Of course I was going with you. I've known Jackson as long as I've known you, remember?"

"Thanks."

"You going to be okay tonight? I mean—"

"Yeah, yeah. I'm going to clean out the house and...and put his stuff up. I'll be fine."

"Well, call me if you're not. You can have dinner with us. Paul has requested pork chops."

"Thanks, but I'll be fine."

Although a few minutes later when she pulled into her own driveway, she wasn't so sure. Snow blanketed the short walkway and porch and she found she was dreading going inside. There would be no one to welcome her home, no tail thumping on the floor, and no whimper of greeting. There would be an empty spot by the fireplace where Jackson spent most of his time these last few months. And there would be the empty food bowl and the scattering of toys that Jackson no longer played with.

"I'm sorry, boy," she whispered. It was the hardest thing she'd ever had to do. But he couldn't get up anymore, couldn't walk. She carried him outside to do his business, then back inside where he spent his day until she came home again. She'd tried leaving him outside, thinking he'd enjoy lying in the sunshine, but that lasted two days. On the second day, she'd come home to find he'd pulled himself by his elbows—which were ripped and bloody—up near the steps of the deck, as if he was trying to get to his old dog bed by the door. It nearly broke her heart to see him like that. So another visit to the vet and more steroid shots to try to get his hips working again—the last resort.

But that wasn't the last resort. The last resort was putting him down. Which she'd done this morning.

And as another wave of tears and guilt hit her, she got out of the truck and hurried through the snow, pausing to stomp her boots on the mat before going inside. When she closed the door on the cold, her eyes automatically were drawn to the blanket by the fireplace. Next to it lay the old stuffed bear that Jackson used to chew on. It no longer had eyes or a nose, and one ear was hanging by a thread, but it was as much a part of Jackson as anything. She bent down and picked it up, her hand squeezing the worn toy as she stared where the eyes used to be. She could get rid of his things—his bed—but she knew she'd never get rid of Mr. Bear.

"You're pathetic," she whispered, and she was glad there wasn't anyone there to see her. Of course, that thought struck her as funny. There hadn't been anyone *there* in so long, she rarely even thought about it anymore.

She tossed Mr. Bear on the sofa and shrugged out of her coat, hanging it on the peg behind the door. She grabbed the remote and turned on the TV, just for some noise. She couldn't stand the emptiness of the house. Even though he could no longer follow her around like he used to do, at least just knowing he was there, by the fire, was enough. At least she wasn't alone.

Standing in the kitchen, she tucked her blond hair behind her ears, doing a mental inventory of her pantry and fridge. Nothing appealed to her. For a second, she thought about calling Tina and taking her up on the offer of pork chops, but the kids would want to know all about Jackson, and she just wasn't up to it.

She sighed heavily. What little appetite she had vanished as she contemplated a can of soup for her dinner. Instead, she turned away, going back into the living room and pulling on her jacket again. Snow or not, she couldn't stay here alone.

Not tonight.

CHAPTER TWO

Despite the snow, the bar was packed. Or maybe it was because of the snow. The first major storm of the year produced excitement in most, and Morgan could imagine the locals crowded around the bar and pool tables, talking about how deep it was out at their place. Seven years and she still didn't know why people got excited by the white stuff. She hated it. Hiking came to an end, replaced by the blasted cross-country skis. Roads became nearly impossible to drive on. It would take a good two hours to get to Gunnison now if you had shopping to do. And with the snow came an end to weekend tourists, campers and hikers. And for her, that meant an end to any possibility of spending the night with a warm body instead of a book…or a toy.

She smiled as she found a parking spot, glad her sense of humor hadn't left her. Actually, even *with* the summer tourists, she could still count on one hand the number of times another woman had shared her bed. Lake City, Colorado, wasn't a retreat for lesbians, she'd found. Not single ones, anyway.

"Hey, Morgan," Jeff called to her as he hurried past with a tray loaded with burgers and beer.

She nodded in greeting and went to the bar, smiling as Tracy had already filled a mug and slid it along the smooth surface toward her.

"Didn't think you'd show up tonight," Tracy said as she wiped a water spot on the bar. "Sorry to hear about Jackson."

"Yeah. But it was time." She took a sip of the cold beer. "Great, thanks."

"You want a burger?"

"No. This is fine. I just wanted out of the house for awhile."

Tracy nodded. "You've come to the right place for distraction. The first storm of the year, they all get a little crazy."

And it was loud and boisterous in the bar, the country music of the jukebox just barely drowning out the slap of balls on the pool table, yet not loud enough to muffle the conversations and laughter that filled the room.

She knew everyone there, some better than others, but after seven years, there weren't many new faces and Sloan's Bar was *the* hangout in town. Whether it was breakfast or lunch, when the bar became the café, or afternoons and evenings, when the dinner menu consisted of burgers and chicken, and the once-a-week steak special, if you wanted to see someone, to socialize, you came to Sloan's Bar.

Which was why Morgan was there now. To socialize. To see familiar faces. To hear familiar stories. And to drink a beer or two and waste a couple of hours. She spun around on the barstool, watching the activity in the bar, smiling as Phil and Buddy argued over a shot in pool. When her gaze landed on a stranger, a woman, she paused, staring. It wasn't often a lone woman ventured into the bar. Especially on a weekday evening long after tourist season had ended.

As she stared, the woman turned, meeting her gaze. Morgan's eyebrow rose. She'd recognize that look anywhere. But even though the woman was attractive—with just a bit too much makeup for her liking—Morgan turned back to the bar. She wasn't in the mood to flirt and make small talk with a stranger. Not tonight.

"Another beer, Tracy," she said, motioning to her empty mug. But before she could take a sip, she felt a presence beside her. She turned, not surprised to find the woman standing there, a smile on her face.

"And here I thought I was coming to the boondocks. Imagine my surprise to find a very attractive woman in this heterosexual hellhole."

Morgan drew her brows together. "Heterosexual, yeah. But hardly a hellhole." She smiled. "You obviously have not tried their double-battered fried chicken."

"I don't eat in places like this. But I was in the mood for a drink," she said, holding up her glass which now contained three melting ice cubes. She shook it teasingly.

Morgan took the hint. "Tracy, how about another over here?"

"May I sit?" the woman asked.

"Of course."

"Scotch on the rocks. Here you go," Tracy said, eyeing the stranger suspiciously.

Morgan winked at her, then turned to the woman. "Where are you from?"

"New York."

Morgan's eyebrows shot up. "On a Wednesday night in November after an all-day snowstorm? I'll assume you're stranded here?"

"Of my choosing." The woman leaned closer. "So, what does one do for fun around here?"

"One?"

"If it is female company you desire?"

Morgan laughed. "They make toys for that sort of thing."

"What? Are you the only lesbian in a hundred-mile radius?"

Morgan nodded. "Feels like it. Although there's a college in

Gunnison, so we're not totally barren in the area."

"And do you raid the sorority houses?"

"Not anymore, no. They keep getting younger and I keep getting older."

"Then professors, perhaps?"

Morgan nodded. "On occasion." But her lone dalliance with a professor ended nine months ago. She knew Stephanie wasn't the woman of her dreams, but after six months of dating, she thought it was at least monogamous. Unfortunately, Stephanie had a weak spot for young college students, Morgan learned. It still smarted to know she'd been tossed aside for a twenty-year-old jock.

The woman leaned closer. "I'm free this evening." She laid a casual hand on Morgan's arm. "In case you're tired of playing with toys," she purred.

Oh, my. A sexual proposition within ten minutes. Must be a record. Morgan flicked her gaze to Tracy, hoping she hadn't heard. She smiled at the stranger, wondering what she wanted. She was attractive. Tall and thin. A little too thin. And her clothes hinted at wealth. What was she doing in Lake City?

And why is she hitting on me?

But Morgan shrugged. Maybe this was what she needed. Mindless sex for one night. Why not? The last woman to share her bed she'd also picked up here at the bar. Not that either of them remembered it the next morning, and thankfully, the woman had hooked up with her camping buddies and had moved down to Pagosa Springs. Morgan had been shocked to learn the girl was only nineteen. That was in June.

"What do you say?"

Morgan drained her beer and set the mug down. She nodded. "Okay. Sure." She got up, motioning to the door.

"I'll follow you," the woman said. "I'm assuming you live alone."

Morgan was about to say, no, there was Jackson waiting for her at home. The reality hit hard. "Yes. I live alone."

Maybe she should reconsider. She wasn't sure she was up

for a night of passion. But after a slow, snowy drive through the tiny town, Morgan didn't have time to consider her actions. She didn't have time to consider much of anything. The woman was on her in a flash, holding her up against the door, her hands at her breasts.

"I like it rough," she said as she kissed Morgan fiercely.

"Rough?" Morgan said weakly, then her eyes widened as the woman's hand slipped inside her pants.

"I'm going to take you places you've never been before," she whispered into Morgan's ear.

Surprisingly, Morgan wanted to go to those places. She relaxed, giving in to her demands, shocked by how ready she was when the woman entered her. She gasped, her hips rocking against this stranger's hand. She groaned loudly as the woman bit down hard against her neck.

"That's it. *Ride* me. Feel me so deep inside you. Oh, yes, you're so wet. *Ride* me," the woman chanted in her ear. "Then you can fuck me just as hard. You can fuck me all night."

Morgan came instantly.

CHAPTER THREE

Morgan lifted her head slowly, afraid to open her eyes. When she did, she sighed with relief. She was alone.

"Good God," she mumbled as she rolled over. She was on the wrong end of the bed, covered only by a sheet. The quilt and comforter had been thrown to the floor. She stared at the ceiling, wondering if she'd be able to walk.

Yeah. She got fucked by a stranger, all right. Fucked in more ways than she could imagine. Her mouth tasted like sex. The room smelled of sex. She closed her eyes and moaned, too tired and sore to move. Even the cold couldn't put her in motion. But she needed to get up. Jackson would want breakfast.

Her eyes opened again.

"No. No Jackson."

She turned her head into the pillow. That's why she had a stranger over last night, she reminded herself. Because there was no Jackson. She finally sat up, groaning again as her muscles protested. She squinted at the clock that had been knocked to the floor. It was already after seven.

"Christ, what was I thinking?" She swung her legs over the side of the bed, wincing at the ache between her thighs. She looked down, seeing the red bite marks. Then she felt her neck, touching the swollen flesh. *A vampire?*

She grinned. *No. Just a biter.*

But her grin faded when she looked at herself in the mirror. She looked like she'd been assaulted. She bent closer to the mirror, rubbing at the blood on her ear. Her neck was littered with bite marks and bruises, as were her breasts. Thankfully, both her nipples were still intact.

"Who the hell was she?"

"What the hell happened to you?"

Morgan shook her head. "Nothing."

"Did you get into a fight or something?"

"Yeah. Something."

She walked away, heading to the coffeepot. Charlie followed.

"Seriously, Morgan. You look like hell."

Morgan took a sip of the strong black coffee, looking at her boss across the rim. "I didn't sleep last night. At least I don't think I did."

"Because of Jackson?"

A ghost of a smile touched her lips. "Yeah. Because of Jackson."

"You could have taken the day off, you know. They haven't even cleared all the roads yet."

"I know. But I didn't want to be at home." She looked at the empty desk by the door. "Where's Berta?"

"Oh, I told her to stay home. She lives down past Turner's Bend, you know. They won't plow that road until later."

"How much did we get?"

"Ten or twelve inches. Got a good base going. Another

snowfall like that and the trails will be ready for snowmobiles." He went into his office, his desk as cluttered today as it had been seven years before when she'd first met him. She was certain some of the same papers had been lying there for years.

"Not much going on today, Charlie. Why don't we clean your desk, huh?"

"Leave my desk alone. Hell, I know where everything is."

"No. Berta knows where everything is." Morgan sat down opposite him, pointing to the clutter. "You never look at this stuff. Why don't you at least put it in a pile?"

"September. Then you can put this crap into any kind of pile you want."

"That's the day, huh?"

"Yep. I'll finish out August. I figure twenty-eight years in the business is enough."

Morgan nodded. "Won't be the same around here."

"No. But I think I'm going down to your neck of the woods."

"Florida?"

"Yeah. Going to buy a trashy travel trailer and park it on the beach," he said with a laugh. "I love to fish too much to be away from water."

And she could imagine him doing it. He was sixty-two years old but could easily pass for ten years younger. He was fit and tan, a true outdoorsmen. And he'd be right at home on the beach.

"You plan on hooking up with a rich widow woman?"

He shook his head. "I did rich once. The rich have too many problems."

Morgan tilted her head. "How come we never talk?"

"We talk all the time. What'd you mean?"

"I know you were married years ago. Didn't know she was rich. You say you have a daughter, but we've never met her, never even seen a picture."

"No?"

"Nope."

"So why do you bring it up now?"

15

"Why do you think?"

He leaned back in his chair and propped his boots on his desk, folding his arms behind his head. "I see Berta's peeked into my e-mail again," he said. "I'm not used to a woman being around. I'm certainly not used to a daughter."

"How old is she?"

He raised his eyebrows. "Thirty-ish, maybe."

"Maybe? You don't know?"

"I haven't really been a part of her life. Kinda lose touch with dates that way."

She nodded. "So what's with the visit now?"

He shrugged. "She called me up and said she had a ski trip planned to Crested Butte. Wanted to know if she could drop by, that's all."

"And are we going to finally get to meet her?"

"Yes. In fact, I think she's going to swing by today. Or else next week when she heads back. I didn't talk to her this morning." He dropped his feet to the floor and scooted closer to his desk. "After dinner last night, she said she wanted to see the sights." He laughed. "I told her there wasn't much to see after dark, but I guess she found something. I didn't hear her come in until three this morning."

Morgan looked away quickly, her mind racing. *Who the hell did I sleep with?* "So she's here alone? Didn't bring a boyfriend?"

"No, she's dating some would-be politician but he didn't come. To hear her talk, they're about to get married. But this is a ladies only trip," he said.

Morgan grabbed the bridge of her nose and squeezed. "I see." *Oh, dear Lord, say it isn't so.* "So, your daughter, what does she look like?" she asked as casually as possible.

"Mona. Her name is Mona. And she's pretty. Tall and thin. Dark hair. Wears too much makeup if you ask me, but that's her thing."

Morgan nodded. Mona. *Moaning Mona.*

I am so dead.

CHAPTER FOUR

"Lake City?" Reese Daniels glanced around. It looked deserted save for the handful of cars parked along the curb. Definitely no shops or restaurants, no blinking neon lights, no laughter of tourists. "My God, is this the town?"

A man cleared his throat behind her and she turned.

"Need some help there, ma'am?"

She nodded. "Sheriff's Office?"

"Down on the corner there," he pointed. "Problem?"

"Definitely," she murmured as she walked away, her boots clicking on the wet sidewalk. Definitely a problem. Lake City wasn't Winter Park. There were no ski slopes, no cute women in colorful jackets and tight pants, and no nightlife. She paused and allowed a small smile. And no mayor's wife. "Ahh, the good old days."

She opened the door, surprised as a bell jingled overhead to signal her arrival. That would be the first thing to go.

"Good afternoon. How may I help you?"

Reese pointed to the bell. "What are we? A convenience store?"

"I beg your pardon?" The older lady stepped from around the desk and regarded her. "Are you Reese Daniels?"

"Yeah. Lose the bell." She walked up to the counter, which was impeccably neat and organized. And why wouldn't it be? She doubted much ever happened here in Hinsdale County. How could it? Most of it consisted of mountain passes without any roads. *A year in purgatory*.

The woman looked at the bell, then back at Reese. "But Ned—Sheriff Carter—liked the bell. That bell's been there for twenty years."

Reese nodded. "I see. And what's your name?"

"Eloise." She smiled. "Nice to meet you."

"Right. So lose the bell, Eloise." She turned. "And my office would be where?"

"Oh. It's in there." She pointed. "But right now—"

"Who's in my office, Eloise?"

"That's Googan. He's kinda been acting—"

"Like the sheriff," Reese finished for her. She walked to the door and knocked on the inside wall. "Hey."

Googan looked up from the newspaper he was reading and frowned. "What are you doing back here? Eloise?" He stood. "You're not supposed to be back here, ma'am."

"*Deputy* Googan, I'm Reese Daniels. And I believe it's *you* who is not supposed to be back here." He had the grace to blush as he shuffled out of the office.

"So you're the *temporary* sheriff? We thought the snow might hold you up for a day or so."

"I've seen snow before."

"We told them we didn't need a temporary sheriff. We told them we could handle it."

"I'm sure you did." She turned to face him. "Trust me. I want to be here far less than you want me here."

"I've been working for Ned nine years. I know the ropes. I

know the people here. I know the country. There's not anything you can do better than me," he said.

Reese smiled. "Apparently your county commissioners thought differently. Something about *real* experience, training, that sort of thing." She shrugged. "That's different than being a deputy in a tiny little town, Googan."

"I'm just saying, I've put in my time. We'd be fine without you. That's all."

Pompous, arrogant ass. She flung the backpack she carried into the chair. "You ever been shot at? You ever busted up a drug deal? You ever pulled your weapon and taken a life?" Her eyes narrowed. "You ever delivered a goddamn baby at two in the morning?"

He slowly shook his head.

"Yeah. That's what I thought." Then she surprised them by laughing. "Not that I expect we'll be doing any of those things here in Hinsdale County." She leaned to look out the window, pulling the miniblinds apart. "So, Googan, how many deputies we got?"

"Two."

She stood and sighed. "Two? That's it?"

"Well, there's not a whole lot of ground to cover in the county, Sheriff."

She shook her head. "Don't call me Sheriff."

Eloise looked from Googan to Reese. "What should we call you then? I mean, what did they call you at your other job?"

"Chief."

Eloise frowned and Reese pulled out the chair with her foot. "I was Chief of Police. Winter Park. So they called me Chief." She sat down. "Call me what you want, Eloise, I don't care. Although I'd prefer it not be bitch or anything like that."

Eloise grunted and left the office. Googan smiled apologetically. "I didn't mean anything by all that. I mean, it's just, Ned had been here for so long. Me too. We just assumed—"

"I understand."

"And you know, come election time next year, I'll be running

19

for sheriff."

"It's all yours, Googan. Trust me. As soon as my time is up, I'm gone."

"Why did you take this assignment then?"

"Take it?" She laughed humorlessly. "No, Googan. I didn't *take* it. Let's just say it was forced on me and leave it at that."

She spun in her chair, turning her back on him. She finally heard him leave. *Great, Daniels. Why don't you piss off the staff in the first five minutes?*

"Okay, I think I will," she murmured. She took a deep breath and let it out slowly. A year and a week. That was her sentence. She was free to leave *next* November. *Damn the mayor's wife.*

CHAPTER FIVE

"Top of the morning to you, Morgan," Sloan greeted her.

Morgan frowned. "What the hell? You Irish today, Sloan?"

He nodded as he filled her coffee cup. "The wife's idea. Flavored coffee," he said.

She took a sip and grimaced. "Where's my plain old roast, Sloan?"

"Irish cream."

"How many people have you run off with this coffee so far?"

He bent closer. "I have to give you one cup of this first, then we'll go to the regular."

She sipped again. "I guess it could grow on you." She glanced to the kitchen. "I feel like a full breakfast this morning."

"Sausage or bacon?"

"Bacon."

"Toast or pancakes?"

"Toast."

"Hash browns or—"

"Hash browns and two eggs, over easy." She rolled her eyes. After seven years, they *still* had this conversation.

He topped off her coffee cup again. "You hear about the new sheriff?"

She shook her head. "You mean we won't be subjected to Googan for a year?"

He laughed. "No. But some woman."

Her eyebrows shot up. "A woman?"

"A real hellcat, to hear Googan tell it." He leaned closer. "The bitch from hell, that's what he said."

"Great. Just what we need." She set her cup down. "I'll have Berta get the scoop from Eloise," she said. She smiled as he went to place her order. Small towns. A curse and a blessing. You could usually find out anything about anybody just by going through Berta and Eloise. Of course that meant your life was also an open book. Which made her wonder how long it would be before someone brought up *Moaning Mona*.

Morgan sat at her desk and did what she always did after the first major storm. She made a listing of the most popular cross-country trails and snowmobile routes and made notes on which ones she still needed to mark. Every summer, before the seasonal staff got laid off, she had intentions to get the trails marked for skiing long before the first snowfall. And each year, that plan fell through. So she was forced to strap on skis and hit the trails herself.

She hated cross-country skiing. But the snowmobile routes? Oh, yeah, now that was fun. She intentionally left those for last, waiting until a good base was down before attempting those in the backcountry. But since the storm a week ago, they'd only had a dusting. The snow had all but melted in the lower elevations.

"Hey," Berta called quietly across the room. "Take a look," she said, motioning to the street.

Morgan inwardly groaned. Moaning Mona was walking beside Charlie, heading this way. She gripped the edge of her desk hard, trying to decide how she was going to play it. She tried to act as nonchalant as possible, only giving the approaching couple a cursory glance. Maybe Moaning Mona wouldn't remember her. Or maybe if she showed indifference, Mona would think Morgan didn't remember *her*.

Yeah, good luck with that.

She kept her head down when the door opened, feigning interest in her trail map. But it would just be rude to totally ignore them. She finally glanced up and offered a quick smile.

"Berta, Morgan," Charlie began. "This is my daughter. Mona."

Mona politely shook hands with Berta then turned with a wicked grin to Morgan. "So *Morgan?* Forest ranger, huh? Imagine that."

Morgan coughed nervously. "Yeah, imagine that." She stuck her hand out. "Nice to finally meet you."

Mona laughed. "Yes, it *was* nice to meet you."

Charlie frowned, looking from one to the other, then glancing quickly at Berta. Berta gave him a knowing smile.

Great. Just great. Berta knows. Just a matter of time before Charlie finds out that I slept with his daughter. Morgan wanted to slink under her desk and hide.

"So, you two have already met?" Charlie finally asked.

Morgan cast pleading eyes at Mona who only chuckled.

"Yes, you could say that." Mona turned to her father. "I ran into her at that bar. What's it called? Sloan's?"

Charlie stared at Morgan. "Why didn't you tell me?"

Yeah, Morgan, why didn't you tell him? "Well, Charlie, I didn't know she was your daughter."

"Well, when I told you her name was Mona, surely that rang a bell. I mean, how many Monas are you going to run into at Sloan's?"

"I—" But Morgan closed her mouth. She refused to tell Charlie—in front of Berta, no less—that she'd slept with his daughter and she never even knew her name.

"As I recall, I don't think we exchanged names. Did we?" Mona asked her, that same sickening smile on her face.

Morgan knew she was blushing, and she looked quickly at Charlie, seeing the questions in his eyes as his brow furrowed, then a slight widening of his eyes as he finally put two and two together. Morgan looked away. *Somebody please shoot me now.*

"So…the morning you came home at three," he said, looking at Mona, "was the same morning that Morgan came in here looking like—" He paused, his glance sliding to Morgan. "Are you saying that—"

"I'm not saying anything," Morgan said, grabbing her coat. "In fact, I have, you know, *things* to do. I have lots of things to do. So, it was nice to meet you, Mona," she said as she headed to the door. "I hope you enjoyed your ski trip, and have a safe trip back to New York."

She slammed the door and walked away, not daring to look back into the office. *What are the chances?* She rolled her eyes, making a silent vow to *never* pick up a woman at Sloan's again.

CHAPTER SIX

"So that's her?" Morgan asked Tracy as she slid her beer down the bar.

"Yeah. Doesn't talk to anyone. Just comes in, gets a beer and burger, and leaves."

Morgan surveyed the tall woman who was sitting alone in a booth, her long legs stretched out as she read a newspaper. Dark hair—short and shaggy—a thick wool sweater over a denim shirt, jeans and boots. Cowboy boots.

Morgan smiled smugly. "Wonder how many times she's going to bust her ass with those boots?"

Tracy grinned. "I hear Googan is scared of her."

"Googan is scared of his own shadow. Not that anything ever happens in this county that Googan couldn't handle, I'm still glad they brought in somebody to replace Ned." She glanced at the woman again. "That's assuming she's a real sheriff." She lowered her voice. "Berta tells me she comes from Winter Park."

Tracy nodded. "Googan said she was Chief of Police up there. Said she demanded they call her Chief and not Sheriff."

"Kinda full of herself, huh?"

Tracy leaned closer. "Why don't you go talk to her?"

"Why would I want to do that?"

"I think she's your type."

Morgan laughed. "Oh, no. I think I've learned my lesson about picking up women in the bar."

"Yeah. About that last one. I saw her—"

"Look, let's just forget about that, okay? Because if word got out that—"

"You mean because she's Charlie's daughter?"

"Christ! Does everybody know?"

"Well, gee, Morgan, the place was full that night. Half the town was here."

"Great. And she ended up being a psycho. And straight at that."

"She was cute."

"Yeah, a cute psycho. And she's my boss's daughter."

"You didn't know that at the time." She paused. "*Did* you?"

"No. Hell, I didn't even know her name. I woke up in the morning and she was gone."

Tracy shook her head. "Don't need to know about all that, Morgan. You know my mother already questions our friendship."

"Still? I've been here seven years. You'd think she'd get over it already."

"It would help if I had a boyfriend."

"In this town?"

"I know. I need to get out of here."

"You've been saying that since I met you."

"I just love it here. Best fishing in the Rockies, if you ask me. And now snowmobiling. I mean, I work nights and have all day to play. If I move to a city, or even a nice-sized town like Gunnison, I'm looking at an eight-to-five job. And doing what? I'm a bartender."

"You're fast approaching thirty," Morgan reminded her.

"I know. And still working at my uncle's bar."

"Well, Sloan doesn't have kids. Maybe when they retire, you could buy the joint."

Tracy tossed Morgan the towel and pointed at the water spot from her beer. "I'll tell my mother you said that. She'll be so proud that my ambition is to own a bar that she'll quit harping on me to move to Gunnison and go to college."

"Uh-huh," Morgan said absently, but her attention was drawn to the new sheriff as Jeff brought over a paper bag with her dinner to go. The woman nodded at Jeff but didn't speak. Then she downed the last of her beer, tossed a couple of bills on the table, got up and left. "You're right. She doesn't speak."

"She's kind of mysterious, don't you think?"

"I was going to say brooding," Morgan said. At least that's how it appeared to her. The woman had folded the newspaper earlier and had simply stared off into space, as if contemplating life, not even the occasional slap of the pool balls interrupting her. There was no smile, no expression. And no words as Jeff brought her dinner. Definitely brooding about something.

CHAPTER SEVEN

It was a beautiful morning, clear and bright, and even the ten-degree temperature didn't dampen Morgan's mood. They'd had a couple inches of snow during the night. Not enough to hinder travel and certainly not enough to add to the base on the trails, but enough to cover the ground and trees with picture-perfect snow. These were the times that Morgan could actually admit she liked winter. Not during a driving snowstorm. Not during subzero weather. And definitely not in March and April when a late storm would push spring back yet again. But on days like today, with a crispness in the air, the sun reflecting brightly off the fresh snow, the crystal flakes clinging to the spruce and firs, and the birds and squirrels flitting about, it was nearly perfect.

And it made her miss Jackson. When he was younger, these were the mornings when he'd bound off the back porch and snorkel in the snow, his eyes bright and playful, begging for a quick walk in the woods. And she would oblige, following him along the trail as he chased after squirrels and played in the snow.

Maybe I should get another puppy.

But she shook her head. It was too hard. *Let it go.*

And she did, driving south out of town toward the lake. Lake San Cristobal was one of the largest natural lakes in the state, formed by the Slumgullion Earthflow. The flow was still active, but it wasn't affecting the lake any longer. And the lake itself was one of the most pristine Morgan had ever seen, with a backdrop of fourteen thousand foot peaks. And the view today was spectacular, the high country getting much more snow than they had down in the valley. Above the lodge, the mountains showed nothing but white. She thought the first big group of snowmobilers might come around this week.

She turned where Hines Creek met the Lake Fork of the Gunnison River and saw a familiar truck parked off to the side. She slowed, knowing Ed Wade was probably just fishing, but she wanted to check on him all the same. As she pulled behind his truck, she saw him and another man standing on snow-covered boulders fly-fishing.

She got out of her warm truck and slipped on her parka, trudging her way to the river. Ed saw her and waved.

"Hey, Morgan. Beautiful morning, isn't it?"

"Absolutely. Most people would say too damn cold for fishing though."

"Oh, I promised my uncle, you know. Uncle Dave? This is Morgan. Forest Service."

"Yep," he muttered and continued with his fishing.

Morgan raised her eyebrows.

"He's eighty-eight. Doesn't talk much."

"I ain't deaf though."

Morgan laughed as he moved farther away from them.

"He came up to spend Thanksgiving. You know my mother leaves for the winter about now. They'll be here until Sunday then ride back together." He lowered his voice. "He's feisty, so I like to get him out of the house."

"No doubt. Well, I'll let you get back to your fishing. I saw your truck and wanted to make sure everything was okay."

"Oh, sure. Thanks, Morgan. Have a good one."

"You too, Ed."

She was shivering as she got back in her truck. As far as she knew, Ed fished nearly every single day. He worked as a fishing guide up at Blue Mesa mostly, or along the river here, always knowing the best spots for trout. In the fall, he took hunters up into the high country looking for elk. And in the winter, you'd find him here along the creek, fishing without a care in the world. And most likely, his eighty-eight-year-old uncle was fishing without a license. And out-of-state at that. His mother lived in Arizona during the winter. But Ed was Ed and she wasn't about to call him on it. He was too by the book when it came to his guide trips to bother him now. Besides, it was too damn cold to stand out and write up a citation for no fishing license. So she waved as she drove past, heading up the pass to the lodge.

It was the Monday before Thanksgiving, but already the lodge was filling. Some brought their own snowmobiles, but most of the guests rented them from the lodge. And as she suspected, the backcountry would be filled with sounds of the machines as the season got underway. If she didn't enjoy snowmobiling herself, she'd be dreading this time of year. The quiet of the mountains was spoiled with the roar of engines. But what an exhilaration it was to fly across the snow at breakneck speed. Snowmobiling was a sport she'd picked up after she moved here and embraced wholeheartedly. Cross-country skiing, not so much.

"Hey, Kenny," she greeted Ellen's son. "You full this week?"

"Oh, yes, ma'am. We're completely full. I was out on the trails at daybreak. Got enough snow to let the machines out."

"Good. Your mom around?"

"You'll find her in the kitchen, as always."

Ellen Patterson and her husband Rick started the lodge twenty years ago and built it into a thriving business during the winter months when most of the other rentals closed down. And they did it by offering snowmobiles and trails right off the parking lot. Sure, the trails were all on National Forest land, but Rick had sculpted his own land to blend into the forest, practically right at the snowmobile shed. And with Charlie's help, had secured new trails to hook up with the established Forest Service trails that began closer in town and down by the river.

"Hi, Morgan, thought I heard your voice."

Morgan accepted the cup of coffee Ellen shoved in her hands and found a spot at the bar as Ellen fidgeted about the kitchen. And that's what she did. Fidget. Never still for a minute. Morgan had long ago gotten used to the constant movement.

"I was just out making the rounds," she said as she eyed the fresh baked cinnamon rolls.

Ellen laughed. "Knowing you, you smelled them down at Hines Creek." She slid the plate closer. "Help yourself."

Morgan bit into the warm dough with an audible moan, her tongue sneaking out to grab the icing that had lodged at the corners of her mouth. "I don't know why you won't just open your own café up here. You'd have enough customers from the lodge to keep you busy."

"Sloan would have our ass and you know it. Besides, running a restaurant is hard work. Sloan'll tell you that."

Morgan sipped from her coffee before taking another bite of the roll. "Kenny says you're full this week. Good thing we got a little snow last night."

"Yeah, it made the trails passable down here. If not, Rick would have had to haul them up above Slumgullion to catch the trails. Not to mention shuttling them back. But we advertise snowmobiling, so we have to deliver." She stopped washing dishes, turning with wet hands. "Say, have you met the new sheriff yet?"

Morgan shook her head. "Nope. Saw her at the bar the other night though. But she keeps to herself. I don't know anyone she's actually talked to on a friendly basis."

"She came up here last Friday."

"Really?"

"Just to introduce herself. Very businesslike, but she seemed nice enough. Not like Ned, of course, who never met a stranger. I bet Googan was plenty pissed."

Morgan laughed. It was common knowledge that Googan thought he'd *earned* the job after following around old Ned like a puppy dog all those years. What Googan didn't know was nobody wanted him to be sheriff. Not that he was totally inept or anything. But like Barney Fife, he just wasn't sheriff material. He watched too many movies as a kid, and half the town was afraid he'd shoot somebody for stealing a pack of gum.

"She seemed your type."

"My type?"

"You know."

"Not you too. What? Is the town tired of me being single?"

"Well, I heard about that woman from the other week. Charlie's—"

"Oh, my God! You heard it too?"

"I'm just saying, you really shouldn't pick up strangers. You never know who they're related to. Besides, the sheriff was kinda cute. In an arrogant sort of way."

"Is that possible?"

"Maybe arrogant is not the right word. Indifferent. How's that?"

"You thought she was cute?"

"Yes. Didn't you?"

"I guess. Tall. Almost handsome," Morgan mused. "But she had an air about her. She didn't seem like someone I'd get along with. Too moody or something. I called it brooding."

"Mmm. Well, I was thinking of you when I met her. That's all."

Morgan smiled as Ellen went back to her dishes. The lone lesbian in town and everyone was trying to fix her up. It was one of the things she loved about this community. Sure, everyone knew everyone else's business, but it was almost like one big family. And after a few months of Charlie hauling her around and dragging her out to the bar every night, they'd accepted her as one of their own. And over the years, they'd known about nearly all of her sexual encounters, no matter how discreet she tried to be.

"Thanks for thinking of me, but I can find my own date."

Ellen snorted. "Yeah, that's worked out great for you so far."

Morgan laughed good-naturedly as she left the kitchen.

After making her rounds up past Slumgullion and down along Hines Creek, Morgan was headed back to town by noon. The temperature had risen into the upper twenties, and the snow had turned to slush on the roads. She slowed as she passed Sloan's Café, smiling at the sign in the window. It still amused her. It was Sloan's Café until about two o'clock when it became Sloan's Bar. A compromise between Sloan and his wife. She thought bar was far too sleazy of a name when she was serving up lunch.

Which is what Morgan was stopping for now. Not that she stopped often for lunch. She came enough in the evenings as it was. But today, she saw Googan's patrol truck parked out front. And she was just curious enough about the new sheriff to pick Googan's brain. Because Berta had struck out with Eloise, getting only the barest of details from her. Berta said Eloise was scared of the woman. And after seeing her just the one time, she could understand why.

"Googan, how's it going?" she asked as she sat down beside him at the bar.

"It's going. If you call Chief Daniels riding my ass every damn day *going*, that is."

"The new sheriff?" she asked casually. "Hey, Sloan. I'll just have tea and a grilled cheese."

"No burger?"

She grinned. "No. Had a huge cinnamon roll up at Ellen's." She spread her hands apart. "This big."

"Yeah. I hear she makes the best." He narrowed his eyes. "She serving breakfast up there at her place now?"

"Oh, yeah. You know, free to guests."

"And you, apparently."

Morgan nudged Googan's elbow when Sloan walked off. "So? The new sheriff? How's that working out for you?"

"She's a beast, that's what. Not only do I have to account for every minute of my day, I have to account for every *mile*. She took a look at the budget and our fuel expenses and nearly went through the roof. I told her it's a big county. There's a lot of driving to do."

Morgan bit her tongue. It was a small county with only minimal county roads. The forest roads, that was her area. But maybe Googan was trying to make his case with the newbie and convince her of the vastness of the county.

"Besides, ain't just me on the budget. Carlton gets around too, you know. And Ned, hell, we all know Ned drove all over the damn place."

"Ned's been gone four months," she reminded him.

"I'm just saying, she jumped all over my ass and I ain't the only one driving."

"So, she's not real laid-back, huh?"

"No, she's got a chip on her shoulder about something, or else she's just plain pissed off at the world. Never smiles. Hell, hardly ever talks. Unless she's jumping my ass about something. I swear, it's going to be a long year. Then come election time, we can send her ass packing."

"You talking about the new sheriff?" Sloan asked.

"*Chief* Daniels, not sheriff."

"Yeah, Carlton came in this morning bitching about her. Said she'd cut his hours back."

"I thought he was only part-time anyway," Morgan said.

"He logged about thirty hours," Googan said. "She's got him down to fifteen. Eloise said she might lay him off during the winter and not bring him back until May."

"Well, you have to admit, there's not a whole lot that goes on during the winter, Googan," Morgan said. "Even in the summer, is it necessary to have three?"

"Just because the Forest Service cuts you back to only two positions during the winter doesn't mean law enforcement should follow suit."

Sloan nodded. "Yep. Could have a rash of burglaries or murders. Need to be prepared."

"Yeah, that's what I'm saying."

Morgan and Sloan exchanged amused glances as Googan downed his tea and got up.

"And now I need to get back on the road before she jumps my ass for having lunch." He nodded at them. "See you later."

"Old Ned had been here so long, I don't think he even knew he had a budget," Sloan said. "Maybe it's good to bring in new blood."

"Yeah, well it's certainly put a bee up Googan's ass."

CHAPTER EIGHT

"Go talk to her."

"I will not," Morgan said. "I invited you out so we could visit."

"Just go introduce yourself," Tina said. "She doesn't talk to anyone in town. Even Eloise is scared of her. Go see if you can feel her out."

Morgan grinned. "Feel her out?"

Tina laughed. "Out, not *up*."

But Morgan shook her head. "Look, by all accounts, she's a real bitch. I don't care if she's gay or not, I don't think we'd hit it off."

"Another round, ladies?" Tracy asked as she swung by their table.

"Sure." Tina grabbed Tracy's wrist and pulled her closer. "How much longer will the sheriff be here?"

"Chief Daniels? Oh, her order will be up in a few minutes.

Why?"

"I'm trying to get Morgan to go talk to her."

"Yeah. Good luck. Morgan doesn't think she'll like the chief."

Morgan nodded. "See?"

"Aren't you at all curious about her? I mean, why does she keep to herself so much?"

"She's nice enough when she orders," Tracy said. "Always leaves a tip. Just doesn't talk much."

Tina turned to Morgan. "See? Not necessarily a bitch. Just maybe quiet."

"All right, fine," Morgan said. "I'll go. But you're buying dinner."

Morgan shoved her chair away and walked across the bar to where Chief Daniels sat quietly, flipping a soggy paper coaster in her fingers. Before Morgan could speak, she looked up.

"Your straight friends finally talk you into coming over?"

Morgan laughed. "Yeah. How did you know?"

She shrugged. "You're Morgan, right? Forest Service?"

"Right."

"Reese Daniels," she said, offering her hand.

"Nice to meet you."

"Good. Now we've met. Maybe your friends will leave you alone."

Morgan smiled, unsure of her statement. Was Reese Daniels just being abrupt? Or did she just get dismissed?

"Excuse me, but my dinner is here."

Okay. Dismissed it is.

"Well, have a good evening then."

Reese Daniels only nodded as she reached for her bag from Jeff, leaving Morgan to sulk back to her table where Tina waited with anxious eyes.

"Well? Well?"

"Well what? I met her."

"And?"

"And I met her. Her dinner came and that's that."

Tina followed her gaze as Chief Daniels left the bar. "But was she nice?"

Morgan raised one eyebrow. "I wouldn't really say nice."

"Oh? So she was a bitch?"

Morgan shook her head. "Not really. She was just...aloof. Or what Ellen Patterson called her, *indifferent*."

"I see. So I guess I won't invite her to have Thanksgiving dinner with us then."

Morgan rolled her eyes. "Please. Please say you're not going to try to set us up. *Please*?"

"Why?"

"She's not my type, for one thing."

"Honey, you're thirty-five years old and you live in Hinsdale County. You can't afford the luxury of having a *type*," she said with a laugh.

Reese got into her truck and closed the door, placing her dinner on the seat beside her. She glanced back at the bar once before pulling away. So that was Morgan, the cute ranger she'd seen around town. She hadn't wanted to be nosy and inquire who she was. Small towns being what they were, she knew it would get back to the woman. So she'd waited. Eventually, her name came up. Ellen Patterson up at the lodge had asked if she'd met Morgan yet, had said they'd have a lot in common.

Reese smiled. Meaning Morgan was a lesbian in case she hadn't picked up on that yet. And if she had to guess, living out here, she was probably single. Cute and single. But none of that made any difference to her. She was in exile, serving out her sentence. She didn't want to meet new people, she didn't want to make new friends, and she didn't want to become involved in anyone's life. When her year was up, she was gone. She didn't want there to be any hesitation about that.

And most likely it wouldn't be back to Winter Park for her. But there were other towns and other ski resorts. She had a good record and an impeccable reputation. Except for the little incident with the mayor's wife, that is. But she liked ski towns. She put in her time in the city, some ten years worth. She had no desire to go back. Small tourist towns provided all the excitement she needed. Crime consisted of drunken encounters and the occasional fender bender. So yeah, she could find another job in another tourist town. She had the credentials. And she could only imagine how ready she'd be to get out of tiny Lake City after a year.

But later, as she ate her dinner alone and stared at the fire that burned hotly, she wondered if she could indeed take a year in exile, a year alone. Not that she wasn't used to being alone. She was. But in between being alone, she was used to being with people, walking the streets, interacting with tourists, giving directions. And meeting the occasional willing woman and taking her home. In Winter Park, she didn't leave behind any friends. And in her department, no doubt they breathed a sigh of relief that she was gone. *Dragon Lady*. But it had been home for the last two years, and it was filled with familiar faces. She didn't feel like she was totally alone.

Here? Eloise was scared of her and walked on eggshells around her. Googan was pissed yet terrified of her. Carlton was about to get fired and he knew it. She was on speaking terms with Jeff at the bar, and the girl behind the counter, Tracy. That's it. She knew who Sloan was, the owner of the bar, but she hadn't really spoken to him. She'd heard Charlie's name a few times and knew that he'd been in town some fifteen years working for the Forest Service. And Ellen had let it be known that Morgan had worked there for seven years.

She's just the sweetest girl. I hope you get to know her.

Sweet or not, Reese had no intention of getting to know her.

She was in exile.

CHAPTER NINE

Morgan walked gingerly to her truck, balancing her cup of hot coffee—Irish cream again—with the breakfast taco Sloan had made her try. It was going to be new on the menu so he was giving out some as samples. It smelled good enough, Morgan noted, but doubted many of the old-timers would enjoy it. She carefully opened the door, trying to keep her footing in the ice and snow and not spill her coffee. She sat inside her truck for a minute, putting the heater on high as she unwrapped the taco, a flour tortilla filled with potatoes, eggs and bacon, and smothered in spicy cheese. "Mmm," she groaned. "That's good. That's real good." Okay. So, maybe the old-timers *would* enjoy it. She nodded, making a mental note to let Sloan know how good it was.

She headed down the street, flipping her wipers on as the snow started coming down harder. She'd just picked up her coffee cup when she saw a blur out of the corner of her eye. She had no time to react as she was thrown forward, hot coffee splashing her as her air bags deployed. She leaned back, dazed, then punched at the air bag, trying to get it out of her face. She looked up at the knocking on the passenger side door, seeing Googan's worried face staring back at her. He jerked the door open, his hands visibly shaking.

"Are you okay, Morgan? God, I don't know what happened. I was just pulling out and there you were."

"I'm okay," she said. "What the hell happened? Who hit me?"

His face turned red. "I did."

She looked out her driver's side window, seeing the sheriff's truck plowed into the side of her Forest Service truck. *Great.* "You hit me?"

"And Chief Daniels is going to kill me."

Morgan glared at him. "Not if I kill you first."

"Please, Morgan. No harm, no foul."

"What the hell are you talking about? No harm? My truck is smashed in."

"She'll probably fire me, send me packing. Then what? This is all I have. I can't lose my job, Morgan."

Morgan unhooked her seatbelt, thankful for that habit, at least. She looked at her uneaten taco lying on the floor in a pool of coffee. She was about to tell him to start packing his bags when she swore she saw the hint of tears in his eyes. *Oh, good grief.* She sighed. "What is it you want me to do?"

"Tell her it was your fault."

"You've lost your mind. First of all, any *idiot* can see that you hit me. Secondly, don't you think someone in town saw?" She looked behind him, seeing the breakfast crowd at Sloan's standing on the sidewalk watching. "There'll be witnesses."

"Please, Morgan. I'm begging you." He lowered his voice. "I'm scared of her."

Morgan scooted across the seat to the passenger side, letting him help her out. "I swear, Googan, you will so owe me for this."

"I promise—"

41

"What the hell happened here?"

They both turned to see the flashing eyes of Chief Daniels as she pinned Googan with a stare. "Googan?"

Morgan stepped forward. "Actually, it was my fault," she said. "I was…I was speeding. Just blasting down the road here. Poor Googan couldn't get stopped in time."

Chief Daniels turned those dark eyes on her and Morgan took an involuntary step back.

"Googan had a stop sign."

"And…and I stopped," Googan said. "Yes, ma'am, really, I did."

"But I was going so fast, once he started through the intersection, he just couldn't stop again in time," Morgan finished for him. *God, he will so pay for this.*

Chief Daniels didn't say anything as she watched them. Then she walked around Morgan's truck, surveying the scene. She put her hands on her hips as she stared at Googan's truck, which was still attached to Morgan's. She looked across the bed of the truck to where Morgan and Googan still stood. Morgan swallowed nervously as she watched the snow cling to Chief Daniels's hair. "So you were racing down the street in the ice and snow, and poor Googan here had the bad luck to hit you. Is that what you're saying?"

Morgan nodded. "And really, it was more like I hit him. I mean, he was already out here on the road and I just came barreling down the street there."

"Uh-huh. I see." Chief Daniels walked back around the truck and Morgan was surprised to see a hint of amusement in her eyes. "Googan? You got the camera?"

"What camera?"

"The camera we use to record the scene here."

He shook his head. "I don't have a camera. Do you?"

"So what do you normally do to preserve evidence?"

He scratched his head. "Well, we just write it up on the accident report. And then draw a picture. You know, there's that little box on the form."

Morgan nearly laughed at the look on Chief Daniels's face. "Excuse me, but I have a camera."

Chief Daniels turned and raised her eyebrows.

"In my truck. I carry a camera with me in my backpack," Morgan said. "You can use it if you want."

But she shook her head. "I don't think we should allow the perpetrator of the crime to supply the camera. Just doesn't seem right."

"*Crime?*"

Daniels ignored her as she turned again to Googan. "We got a wrecker service in town or anything like that?"

"Sammy Morris has a small tow truck. He's got the garage down at the end of town," he said.

"Why don't you go over to the office and give him a call? After we get all the insurance sorted out, we'll have two trucks that'll need some body work. Morgan's appears to still be drivable. Yours, on the other hand, looks like it blew the radiator."

"Yes, ma'am. I'll get right on it." Googan took off at a dead run, apparently thankful to leave the scene unscathed. Morgan waited until those dark eyes turned her way.

"So, Morgan, you often drive like a maniac during a snowstorm?"

"Not normally, no."

"Thought today was a good day for it, did you?" She pointed to the two trucks. "Evidence indicates that Googan hit you. No skid marks for either of you."

"It just happened so fast, we didn't have time to stop."

Chief Daniels smiled quickly. "And that's your story? This accident is your fault?"

"Yes."

"Okay, then. Let's write up an accident report." She pointed to her truck, which was parked behind Morgan's. "We can get out of the snow," she said as she ran a hand through her hair, shaking the snow from it.

Morgan nodded, then waved at Sloan, motioning him and the others to go back inside. She went around to the passenger

43

side and got inside Chief Daniels's truck, rubbing her hands together to keep them warm. She waited while the chief searched her console, finally pulling out a small clipboard and what she assumed was the accident form.

"Okay, let's start with the easy part. Let me see your driver's license."

Morgan gave a quick, embarrassed smile. "I don't actually have it with me."

"You don't carry your driver's license with you?" She shook her head. "Your traffic fines are just piling up, aren't they?"

"I don't see the point. Everybody knows me here."

"Do you at least know your number?"

Morgan bit her lip. "No."

Chief Daniels sighed, then tapped the form. "Okay. Name. Morgan what?"

"Morgan's actually my last name. Everyone just calls me *Morgan*."

"I see. Then what's your first name?"

Morgan bit her lip again. "I'd rather not give you that information."

"Excuse me?"

"I just don't see that it's necessary. I mean—"

"You do understand that I have to file an accident report, right?"

"Look, why do we have to have all this formality? I mean, we had a little accident. Nobody got hurt."

Chief Daniels tapped the form with her pen again. "See this? Accident report. Makes this *little accident* official. It's not a matter of whether you want to complete it or not. It's kinda required by law."

Morgan took a deep breath. "Okay, off the record?"

"No, not off the record. This is an accident report. It'll have to be filed with the insurance claim." She narrowed her eyes. "Now what's your name?"

Morgan lifted her chin up defiantly. "M period. Z period. Morgan."

"You have initials for names? Come on."

"It's a possibility."

"Shame you don't have your driver's license to prove it. But you're trying my patience, Morgan. M stands for what?"

Morgan leaned closer, her face only inches from Chief Daniels. "If you so much as breathe a word of this," she threatened. "I'll…I'll…" She didn't blink, but Morgan could swear she saw a ghost of a smile cross her face.

"Name?" she repeated.

"Marietta."

Chief Daniels laughed. "All of that for *Marietta*? I thought it was going to be something hideous." She tapped the form again. "Middle?"

Morgan pursed her lips. "Z." *Good God, why haven't I had my name legally changed?*

"Are we going to have to go through all of this again?"

"Why do you need a name?"

"Because the form asks for a name. It doesn't ask for an initial. It asks for a name." She held the clipboard up. "See?"

"God, I swear," Morgan muttered. She pointed her finger at Chief Daniels. "You think I'm kidding, but I'm not. If *anyone* in this town *ever* calls me by these names, I will hunt you down."

"Are you threatening a peace officer?"

"Call it what you want." This time Chief Daniels did laugh and Morgan relaxed a little.

"Okay, Miss Morgan, please tell me your middle name. I promise I won't tell a soul."

"Oh, dear God, I can't believe I'm about to do this."

"Can it be that bad?"

"My father's mother died three weeks before I was born. Her name was Marietta. Then my mother's mother died two days before I was born. I'm sure it's what sent her into labor. They scrapped the names they'd picked. Normal names. I could have been Jennifer. I like Jennifer. And they had Melanie picked out. I could live with Melanie. But no, they felt the need to name me after them." She took a deep breath. "Her name was…*Zula*,"

45

Morgan finished in a whisper. Again, the twitch of a smile from the sheriff.

"Zula?"

"Shh! Not so loud," Morgan said, quickly looking out the windows at the handful of onlookers.

"You're telling me no one in town knows your name?"

"And I'd like to keep it that way."

Chief Daniels stared at her, finally putting the clipboard down. "How long are you going to keep up this charade?"

"Not telling anyone my name is hardly a charade. Everyone calls me Morgan. They always have. There's no—"

"I'm talking about this accident. A rookie cop with no training could tell Googan ran the stop sign and hit you. I want to know why you're covering for him."

Morgan leaned back against the seat and let her breath out. Yes, like she'd told Googan. Even an idiot would know. And apparently Reese Daniels wasn't an idiot.

"He was afraid you'd fire him."

"And so you agreed to lie for him?"

"I didn't want to but he looked so scared. I mean, I thought he was going to start crying. And really, no one was hurt."

They both looked up as Sammy Morris drove past them in his dilapidated old tow truck.

"How far were you going to go with this lie? I mean, were you going to file a false insurance claim? Have the government pick up the tab for the accident?"

Morgan looked at her, speechless. She hadn't actually thought that far ahead.

"That part didn't cross your mind, huh?"

"No."

"Okay, give me your real statement please. I'll have Eloise file it with the county's insurance."

"Eloise? Oh, no. She can't possibly see the accident report."

"And why not?"

"If she finds out my name, the whole damn town will know." She pointed out the window at the onlookers. "I know you haven't been here long, but surely you've realized by now that the source of the town's gossip is Eloise and Berta."

"And Berta would be who?"

"She's Charlie's secretary. They're childhood friends, born and raised around here. And there's not a thing that goes on in town that they don't know about." She motioned with her head. "See Eloise standing over there by Stella's Beauty Shop? That's Berta beside her."

"Why in the hell is everyone out in the street?"

Morgan smiled. "It's been two years since we've had a fender bender. This'll hold them for a week or so, especially when they find out I tried to take the blame for Googan because he's scared of you."

"Is he really scared of me?"

"Most of the town is scared of you. It's not like you're Miss Congeniality."

"And he thought I was going to fire him?" She smiled. "Good."

CHAPTER TEN

Morgan stomped her boots on the mat before going inside. She smiled sheepishly at Berta. "I'm fine," she said before Berta could ask.

Berta motioned to Charlie's office. "He wants to see you."

"Does he know?"

"About the accident or the cover-up?"

Morgan rolled her eyes. "There was no cover-up. I was—"

"Lying for Googan." Berta shook her head disapprovingly. "And yes, he knows."

"I swear," she mumbled. *Nothing* in this town was a secret. She paused at his door and he looked up from the newspaper he was reading. He folded it neatly and pointed to the visitor's chair. She swallowed nervously, then sat down. It wasn't the accident she was worried about. It was *Mona*. Charlie hadn't mentioned a word about his daughter since the little scene in the office the other day. In fact, Charlie had pretty much avoided her. And she him.

"Are you okay?"

Morgan nodded. "Yes, just a little fender bender. Nothing serious."

"And the false statement Berta said you gave?"

"Oh, good grief." Morgan rested her elbows on her thighs and leaned forward. "Googan about peed in his pants. He was afraid she'd fire him. I mean, you should have seen him. He begged me to take the blame."

"I know," Charlie said with a laugh. "The chief already called me."

"She *told* on me?"

"I think she was just making sure I knew the department wouldn't be held liable. And to say that she's not going to fire Googan, although I understand he got his ass chewed out."

Morgan relaxed as she sat back again. "I'm sorry, Charlie. I thought he was going to start crying." They sat quietly for a moment, the silence lengthening. Finally, she cleared her throat. "You ready to talk about it?"

He folded his hands together on his desk as he stared at her. "I've decided it's not any of my business." When Morgan would have spoken, he held up his hand. "Not that I pretend to understand any of this. I mean, she's practically engaged. But she told me she likes to—"

"Sleep with women," Morgan finished for him.

"I just don't get it. Do you?"

"No. No, I don't. But, Charlie, I had no idea she was your daughter. It was the day Jackson died. I had to get out of the house. And she was at the bar. In all fairness, she came on to me. I didn't—"

"I don't need to know all the details, Morgan."

"Well, I'm just saying—"

"It doesn't matter. She's gone. And I doubt we'll ever see her again."

"Oh, no. Because of *me*?"

Charlie laughed. "Not because of you, Morgan. That's just

the kind of relationship we have. Hell, I never got more than a picture until she was twenty-two and she decided to seek me out. But you know, we don't have anything in common. We knew that the first time we met…what, ten years ago? A few phone calls here and there didn't change that. Honestly, I was as surprised as anyone that she wanted to come visit me." He stood and went to the window, looking out. "Nothing's changed. I'm just basically a sperm donor. I'm not her father." He turned back around. "You've been more of a daughter to me than she has, Morgan."

"Oh, Charlie. I'm sorry."

"No, don't be sorry. That's just the way it is. Her mother, well, she just married me to piss off her parents. She had already moved back home by the time Mona was born."

"So you didn't get custody at all? Visitation?"

"I got paid off to disappear, Morgan. It's not something I'm proud of, but hell, they made it clear I wasn't going to be a part of the kid's life. They know where I've been. They sent pictures. The kid out on a yacht, her on a pony, her playing tennis at the country club. That kind of stuff."

"That's sad, Charlie."

He shrugged. "That's just the way it is. So even though we've got the same blood, we're not the same people. Like I said, we don't have anything in common, just like I didn't have anything in common with her mother."

"So she just went back to New York?"

Charlie grinned. "Back to her fiancé. Poor bastard."

Morgan laughed, then got up and went around to him, hugging him quickly. "Thank you for not being mad at me. For that, and well, for the accident."

"Speaking of that, you're going to need something to drive while your truck is being fixed. Why don't you hit up Alpine Rentals for a Jeep?"

"A Jeep? Seriously?"

"County is picking up the tab, not us."

"Oh, cool. Thanks, Charlie."

CHAPTER ELEVEN

"So let me get this straight," Tina said. "In the last two weeks, you've managed to pick up a strange woman here at the bar, then you find out she's Charlie's daughter, of all people. Then Googan runs into you because he never stops at that damn stop sign. And then you *lie* for him so he doesn't get into trouble?"

Morgan sipped her beer and merely nodded.

"Charlie's *daughter*? What were you thinking?"

"Obviously, I didn't know she was his daughter, and keep your voice down. The whole town doesn't need to know."

Tina laughed. "Yeah, keep thinking no one knows."

"It's so embarrassing."

"And it should be." She lowered her voice. "Berta said she was engaged."

Morgan nodded. "That's what I hear."

"Then why would she *do it* with you?"

"I know you don't understand this," Morgan said, then

grinned. "But sex with a woman is pretty amazing. In fact, I called her *Moaning* Mona."

"Stop. Gross. Too much information," Tina said with a laugh.

"In other words, I wasn't the first woman she's been with," Morgan said. "Because she knew exactly what she was doing." She, too, lowered her voice. "She was a biter."

"A what?"

"You know, a biter."

"During sex?"

"Yeah."

Tina again shook her head. "I don't want to know about it. I don't even want to *think* about it."

"Thankfully, Charlie wasn't pissed about it."

"Yeah, Berta said you had a talk with him."

Morgan tapped the table. "Why must that woman tell everything she knows? Can't I be the first to tell news that involves *me*?"

"No. And you should be used to it by now." Tina waved Tracy down and held up two fingers. "I'll stay for one more," she said to Morgan. "I want to hear about the sheriff."

"Chief Daniels? What about her?"

"I heard you were locked in her truck for nearly a half hour. And you were arguing."

Morgan rested her chin on her palm, shaking her head. "I swear, this town. No, I was not *locked* in her truck. She was taking my statement and it was snowing, so we sat in her truck."

"Is this the statement where you were lying?"

"Until she told me that she knew I was lying, yes."

She shoved her empty mug aside and folded her hands on the table. "So, what was she like?"

"Who?"

Tina grinned wickedly. "You know who. Chief Daniels."

"She was, well at first, it was all business and she was abrupt, perhaps even a little arrogant. She lightened up some, but I'm not sure I like her. There's something kinda *mysterious* about her. Like Googan said, she's got a chip on her shoulder about something."

"Googan said that because she's acting like a real sheriff and holding him accountable instead of the good old boy way that Ned handled things."

"Yeah, but I can see where she has a bit of an attitude." She waved her hand dismissively. "Doesn't matter. She knew I was trying to cover for Googan and busted me on it. Then I hear she chewed Googan's ass for it."

"At least he's still got a job." Tina smiled as Tracy set two beers on the table for them. "Thanks, girl. Why don't you sit and chat for a bit?"

"Can't. Jeff's not here yet so I have to help with dinner." She touched Morgan's shoulder. "Heard what happened with Googan."

"I don't doubt that."

"He always runs that stop sign. Did you tell the chief that?"

"No, I didn't tell her that. She was plenty pissed the way it was."

"And he deserves it." She looked at Tina. "You having dinner here tonight?"

"Oh, no. Leftovers. But I wanted to come in and get the scoop from Morgan. And why didn't you tell me about Charlie's daughter?"

Tracy winked at Morgan. "Because I didn't think she wanted you to know."

"Since when has that stopped you?"

"You don't have to know *everything*," Tracy said as she walked away.

"You paid her off, didn't you?" Tina said.

"I did not."

"I don't believe you." She took a swallow from her beer. "Are we still on for Thanksgiving dinner?"

"Yeah, but like I said, don't wait for me. The lodge is full and the trails will be packed. It's the first real run of the season." As much as she loved Tina and Paul and their kids, Thanksgiving had become just another day to her, normally because she usually volunteered to be out on the trails to allow others with families to enjoy the holiday. But here in Lake City, it was just her and Charlie during the winter, so she had no choice. Secretly, she liked it that way. First run of the season, fresh snow. She could feel the adrenaline now as she imagined the powerful snowmobile between her legs. She never minded showing up late for dinner after a day on the trails.

CHAPTER TWELVE

Morgan set her beer mug aside and watched as Reese Daniels sauntered into the bar. The sheriff nodded in her direction, then took a seat at an empty booth.

"Same time nearly every night," Tracy said as she took a frosty mug from the freezer and filled it. "I wish you would go talk to her. Nobody talks to her. She just sits there by herself, waiting on her burger."

"I tried talking to her, remember? She's not very friendly." Although during her *accident report*, the sheriff hinted that she might have a sense of humor. Morgan had seen her hide a smile several times. And of course, who wouldn't? Finding out someone's name was *Marietta Zula* surely would bring fits of laughter.

"Maybe she's just shy," Tracy suggested.

"Oh, please. Shy? That woman is not shy." Morgan gazed again at the sheriff. No, not shy. She was too *powerful* to be shy.

And she wasn't sure if she meant physically powerful or not. Her personality was forceful, confident. Powerful. But her stature seemed to be as well. She was a few inches taller than Morgan's five-seven, and although she had not seen her without a jacket or parka on, she imagined her to have a muscular frame.

"I think she's cute."

Morgan pulled her gaze away from Reese Daniels and frowned at Tracy. "Cute?"

"Don't you think so?"

Morgan shrugged. Well, yeah. But cute wouldn't be the word she'd use. She was attractive, not beautiful. She was too masculine looking to be called beautiful. Handsome, yes. But her face had a hardness about it, her dark eyes difficult to read. Maybe that was why Ellen had called her indifferent. She couldn't read her.

But she conceded to Tracy. "She's attractive, yes."

"Then—"

"But not my type," she quickly clarified. The last thing she wanted was Tracy playing matchmaker with the new sheriff. It was bad enough Tina—and even Ellen—had hinted Morgan should become friendly with her.

Tracy laughed. "Do you have a type, Morgan? There was the professor for a while. Definitely not your type. There was the teenager you picked up during the summer. Now she wasn't your type, surely. And most recently Mona. Now don't tell me *she* was your type."

"The teenager was nineteen, posing as twenty-one, and I'd had a bit too much to drink to think clearly. Mona was a *huge* mistake, but I was mourning over Jackson and not thinking clearly. And the professor," Morgan grinned, "she was kinda good in bed, and it was winter."

"And so you weren't thinking clearly."

Morgan laughed. "Not really, no. We had nothing in common, obviously. She got immense pleasure out of using vocabulary that I couldn't pronounce, much less know the meaning of."

"The snooty genius types never make good partners," Tracy stated matter-of-factly.

"So I should stick with the dimwitted sheriff types?"

Tracy took Morgan's mug and filled it, then handed both to her. "Go take her beer over to her and *talk* to her."

Morgan let out a deep breath. *God, all these women trying to set me up!* But she supposed it wouldn't hurt to talk to the sheriff. It would be nice to make a new friend, at least. So she shoved away from the bar, taking both mugs with her as she approached the booth.

"Good evening, Chief Daniels," she said easily. "Tracy asked me to bring your beer over." She slid the frosty mug in front of her.

Reese looked up, her lips twitching in a smile. "Ma-Ma-Morgan," she said.

Morgan's eyes narrowed. "Don't even think it," she said.

Reese laughed. "But who would name their child *Zula*?"

Without thinking, Morgan reached out and grabbed Reese's arm with her thumb and forefinger, twisting hard in a pinch. She accomplished her goal. Chief Daniels let out a yelp that caused everyone in the bar to look their way.

"Jesus Christ!"

But Morgan didn't flinch. "Never *ever* say that word in public again."

"I'm going to have a bruise."

"Good. I hope it hurt."

Reese rubbed her arm. "Is this your normal approach when you're trying to pick up women?"

"Excuse me?" Morgan took a step back.

"Because I'm not interested."

"Oh, my God. You think I want to *sleep* with you?"

"Don't you?"

Morgan laughed and slid into the booth opposite her. "No. Whatever gave you that idea?"

"From what I've gathered, you're the only lesbian in town. And you're single."

"So if you're the only lesbian in town and another one shows up, you automatically think sex? I was thinking more of a friendly bonding. You know, someone to check out the straight chicks with, someone to fight over the occasional ski bum who stumbles into town, that sort of thing. I don't want to *sleep* with you, Chief."

Reese tilted her head. "Why not? Am I not your type?"

Morgan studied her. Yes, definitely attractive. Her hair was just unruly enough to be sexy, her dark eyes intense. But her type? "You're hiding something, and you brood about it," Morgan said. "And not that I don't find you attractive. I do. I mean, I'm not dead," she said with a laugh. She leaned closer. "Why are you here?"

"Here? Here as in Hinsdale County?"

"Yes. Not that we don't appreciate it. After Ned left, we all thought we'd be stuck with Googan."

"And when my year is up, you very well may." Reese took a swallow of beer. "I'm in exile. My prison term is up in one year."

"Oh, yeah? What'd you do? Sleep with your boss's daughter or something?" At the slight blush that colored Reese's face, Morgan laughed. "Oh, my God! Are you insane? What was she? A teenager?"

"Insane? You should know."

"What do you mean by that?"

"Although Charlie's daughter was straight, I hear. I think you trump me, Marietta *Zula*," she said with a wicked grin.

Morgan gritted her teeth. "How do you know about Charlie's daughter?" She leaned closer. "And have you forgotten the pinch? Because I'll do it again."

Reese rubbed her arm. "No, I haven't forgotten."

Morgan touched her warm cheeks, knowing she was blushing. "How do you know about Mona?" she asked quietly.

"Eloise mentioned it."

"Oh, good grief."

"So was she really straight?"

"I don't know. I certainly wasn't her first." Morgan blushed again. "I can't believe I'm telling you about her."

"Isn't that part of our lesbian bonding thing?"

Morgan smiled. "Jackson had just died. I was lonely. I—"

"Who was Jackson?"

"He was my dog. My partner, my friend." Morgan stared into her beer for a moment, remembering Jackson. "Anyway, she was here. I had no idea she was Charlie's daughter. Actually, I can't believe I took her to my house. I don't normally do things like that." Morgan smiled at her. "So what's your story?"

"Not the boss's daughter." She sipped her beer again. "It was his wife."

"Oh, my God, his *wife*?"

"It was actually the mayor's wife."

"Well, I hope it was good."

"Quite good. Just not good enough to lose my job over, no."

"What happened?"

"I had a rather cushy job, Winter Park. Chief of Police." She grinned. "That's where the Chief Daniels thing started. And in my defense, she came on to me. Relentlessly."

"I'm sure."

"It's the truth."

"And you finally gave in?"

"Yeah. Unfortunately, it was at the mayor's house. And he came home unexpectedly."

"Oh, my."

"Of course, he couldn't just fire me. You have to have cause. Sleeping with his wife wasn't justification. And he didn't want the whole county to know. So, he pulled some strings, and here I am. In lovely Lake City, Colorado, in the middle of winter, hours from the nearest town of any size."

"Why didn't you just resign?"

"Why should I? I did a good job. There was no reason to resign. And I need a job."

"You were having an affair with the mayor's wife."

"Affair really isn't the word. And like I said, she came on to me."

"Not being able to say *no* is hardly an excuse."

"I never said it was an excuse." Reese looked up as Jeff brought over her dinner. "Thanks, Jeff."

"Sure thing." He nodded at Morgan. "Another beer?"

She shook her head. "No. I'm heading home. Thanks." She slid to the edge of the booth and stood. "I guess that explains why you've been so standoffish with everyone. It's easier to cut and run after a year when you don't have relationships with the people you're sworn to protect. We're not really *real* that way." She motioned to the window. "Storm coming in tonight," she said. "Ten inches."

"I heard. Ought to be a slow day tomorrow."

Morgan nodded. "Goodnight."

Reese watched her go, then tossed back the last of her beer. She couldn't remember the last time a woman had dared speak to her that way. And the pinch? Damn, that hurt. She smiled slightly. Just because she was in exile didn't mean she had to shun *all* contact with the locals. Morgan was right. It was easier to cut and run. But it would make the year pass more quickly if she had a friend to hang out with, have dinner together occasionally. She arched an eyebrow. *A friend?* No, an acquaintance. She didn't really make friends. She'd been told once that her personality was a little too insensitive and gauche to be conducive to forming friendships. She generally said what was on her mind, and no, she didn't waste time with unnecessary pleasantries. Too many years in the police business for niceties. Too many years of running hookers and druggies off the streets in Vegas. Sweltering in one hundred fifteen degrees would make anyone insensitive to the pleasantries of civilized culture. That, and she found it a waste of time.

So she stood, tossing a few bills on the table, enough to cover her meal and a few extra for a tip. She walked out without speaking to anyone, pausing only to nod in Tracy's direction as she slipped into the night.

CHAPTER THIRTEEN

It was the kind of snowstorm Morgan hated. Not the fast-moving ones that dumped their snow and then moved on, leaving behind brilliant blue skies. No. This was the kind that started during the night and hung around all day, a *make the world a dreary gray, fuzzy with the swirl of snow, bring life to a standstill* kind of storm.

She moved away from the window and back to the fire, holding her hands out unconsciously to the warmth. Yes, she bitched about the cold and the snow. But really, it was the cabin fever brought on by the cold and snow that got to her. She *hated* being confined like this. *Hated it.*

Yeah, yeah, it was pretty and all that after it was over with. It was just getting to that point that wore on her nerves. And to make matters worse, there was no Jackson around to distract her, no one to talk to, no one to take out into the storm for a quick potty break. Being stuck inside her tiny Forest Service house, staring out at the endless snow, made her feel as lost and alone as she'd ever been.

Ridiculous.

They still had power in town. She had a collection of DVDs. She could watch a movie. Or better yet, read a book. But glancing at the bookshelf, she shook her head. *Not in the mood.* So she paced again, back and forth, her eyes darting between the fire and the endless white outside the window.

Reese strolled through the quiet office, not even Eloise bothering to make the drive into town this morning. Reese had always lived by the code that the post office and the police would be ready for duty regardless of the weather. Apparently, that didn't hold true in Lake City. But at least Googan had the good sense to call and offer to come in. Eloise was more to the point. *I guess you know only a fool would try to drive in this mess.*

"And here I am," she muttered as she filled her coffee cup for the fourth time. Even Sloan's was empty, she noted, as she looked out on the deserted street that ran through town.

She'd heard on the scanner that the snowplows wouldn't be out until the storm moved on. At least she'd had the foresight to post the *Road Closed* signs last night heading to Slumgullion Pass. A quick call to the Pattersons up at the lodge confirmed her decision. Rick told her they'd had at least two feet. She also noted the excitement in his voice. Snow meant snowmobilers. It was no different than when she worked in Winter Park and the folks at the resort were all having orgasms as the snow kept falling and falling.

Ah, Winter Park. She smiled as she fondly remembered the town. Ski season doubled the population, and the bars and restaurants were the hub of activity. A storm like today, the place would still be alive with tourists. She pulled her gaze away from the empty street. Not here, no. No tourists. Not even the locals were out and about.

"And a whole year of this," she murmured as she went back to her office to brood.

CHAPTER FOURTEEN

"You want me to what?" Morgan stared at Charlie. He'd obviously lost his mind.

"A couple of hours. It won't be bad."

Morgan glared at him. "Despite the fact that I don't really even like the woman, you want me to cross-country *ski* for a couple of hours? Charlie, you know I *hate* that. Why can't I take her out on snowmobiles?"

"Because she wants to ski, to learn the trails, get familiar with it all before the summer tourist season picks up."

"Christ, Charlie, it's December. She's worried about the summer season already?"

"Look, she requested and I obliged."

"No, you want *me* to oblige." She took a deep breath, already dreading being on those damn skinny skis for hours. But it was a beautiful day. Not even a hint of a breeze, the sky an endless blue, the temperature feeling almost balmy at thirty-five.

"So you'll do it?"

"Do I have a choice?"

Charlie grinned. "I guess you could have pulled your hamstring on your morning jog."

"Funny."

"Seriously, I think it's just being neighborly. Besides, she doesn't really know anyone in town."

"Oh, I'll do it, Charlie." She went to her desk and fished out her keys. "Nothing better than a little cross-country skiing to get your juices flowing." She whipped her head around. "Do not comment on that," she said quickly.

He laughed. "Wouldn't touch it. But you know, this might give you a chance to get to know each other. It never hurts to make new friends, Morgan."

She shook her head. "I don't know about that. She's standoffish, I told you that."

"The last couple of times we talked, she was friendly enough."

"If I see her at Sloan's, she doesn't speak, not unless I make the effort first. I mean, she's been here a month. You'd think she would have lightened up by now," she said as she pulled on her jacket. She paused at the door. "And by the way, you owe me dinner at Sloan's for volunteering me for this. You can pay up on steak night."

Reese stared out her door and through the window to the street, waiting. She had no doubt that Charlie would have to talk Morgan into this. She'd heard from Eloise that Morgan hated skis. Hated winter for that matter. Reese also hated skis and would have loved to take a spin out on snowmobiles. But that's hardly conducive to having conversation and getting to know someone. Which was why she'd come up with this little plan. She was simply bored enough to toss out her *don't get involved* rule.

Bored out of her mind. There was no crime, had been no traffic accidents other than Googan's little mishap, no speeding tickets to issue, no one complaining of a disorderly neighbor, not even a drunken incident over at Sloan's Bar. No crime, no theft, no reports to write up, nothing. Now she knew why the fender bender in town had garnered such interest. It would have to hold them over until tourist season.

That's when she realized that if she didn't find something to do, didn't start having a *life*, then she'd go stark raving mad during her year of exile.

Marietta Zula Morgan seemed to be her only option. She nearly laughed out loud as the name rattled around in her brain, thinking of the pinch Morgan had given her the other day for teasing her about it. Yes, Morgan seemed the logical choice if she was going to attempt to make friends with someone. They were generally the same age, although she suspected Morgan to be a little younger. They were both lesbian, both single. Two qualities there weren't a lot of in the county, she was certain. So she would make an effort. And cross-country skiing seemed like a good choice to start with. They would have some time together, alone. And if they didn't kill each other, the next time she saw Morgan out at the bar, she'd go over and talk. She'd make the effort.

So she waited, tapping her fingers impatiently on the desktop, wondering for the thousandth time why she accepted this *buyout*, why she hadn't just quit her job like the mayor had wanted and moved on, looking for something else. But she knew why. If she quit, then it would follow her.

Why'd you quit your previous position?

Well, you see, there was the mayor's wife…

And if she found another job, it wouldn't be top dog. No, she'd most likely have to settle as deputy in someone else's gig. Something she wasn't willing to do.

And that's why you're stuck in Lake City.

"Chief? Morgan's coming over from across the street," Eloise called. "Are you expecting her?"

She lifted a corner of her mouth in a grin. "Yeah, just send her back." She wiped the smile from her face when she heard that damn bell jingle. Her *lose the bell* speech had fallen on deaf ears. And now after a month, it had grown on her, despite her continued threats to rip it down.

She tilted her head, feigning interest in her computer as she listened to Morgan greet Eloise.

"Beautiful day, isn't it, Eloise?"

"Oh, I'll say. After that storm the other day, I never thought the snow would melt this fast in town."

Reese smiled as she heard the slight pause.

"Is she in?"

"The Chief? Oh, yes. Come on back, Morgan. Is everything okay?"

"Fine, Eloise. Thank you."

Reese looked up as Morgan stood in her doorway, her cheeks red from being outside. Her eyes—a nice shade of blue and green—met hers, one eyebrow arching questioningly.

"Skiing?"

"I'd heard it was a passion of yours," Reese said, unable to hide the smile that sprang to her mouth.

"And busted you are," Morgan said. "Am I being punished for something?"

"You can't hate it that much, surely."

Morgan slumped down into the chair. "It's far too much work to be considered enjoyable, that's all. And why the sudden interest in our trails?"

"I just haven't been *out* yet, that's all. So much beautiful country here, I thought I should take advantage of it."

"The Pattersons rent snowmobiles."

Reese laughed. "You *really* don't like skiing, do you?"

Morgan tilted her head. "I'm not certain if it's skiing or spending a couple of hours with you that's got me hesitant." She leaned forward. "You haven't exactly been very sociable."

"You mean with you?"

"With anyone."

Reese nodded. "You're right. I'm used to being alone and *not* used to making friends." She spread her hands. "But what the hell? I thought I'd give it a try. That is, if you're willing."

Morgan stood. "Fine. But I'll warn you now, I will whine and bitch constantly while we're on skis. And should I fall down off of those damn skinny things, do not make fun of my attempts to get back up."

Smiling, Reese pushed her chair away. "Deal."

CHAPTER FIFTEEN

Morgan paused about halfway up the latest switchback, leaning on her poles and trying to catch her breath. *Goddamn stupid sport.* She glared at Reese who waited patiently beside her.

"We could be on snowmobiles."

"Then we would have missed this lovely hike."

Morgan lifted one pole and whacked Reese on her thigh. "I hate you already."

"It's a beautiful day, Zula. How can you hate me?"

"Oh, my *God!* Do not call me that!" she shrieked as she went after her. And if she could have caught her, she'd have tackled her and beat the shit out of her. As it was, Reese skied safely away, her laughter ringing out in the still air. "I *hate* you," Morgan called after her.

"Now, now."

"I mean it!" But her eyes widened as she felt her balance slipping, her skinny skis teetering dangerously. *Oh, crap.* She closed her eyes as she fell, the cold sting of the snow smashing her cheek. She leaned up on her elbows, blinking several times to get the snow out of her eyes. She heard the swoosh, swoosh of Reese's skis as she came back down the trail toward her. *And isn't this lovely.*

"You okay?"

Morgan chose to ignore the amusement she heard in Reese's voice, instead she focused on her words of concern. "Just peachy."

A pause. "Want me to help you up?"

Morgan bit her lip. "No, no. You've done enough."

"Oh, and now you're going to blame *me* for this little mishap?"

Morgan rolled to her side, trying to keep from twisting her ankle in the process. "Of course you are to blame."

"All because I called you—"

"Do *not* say it!" Morgan swung her pole around and hit Reese again. "You simply infuriate me."

"Oh, now, come on. Let me help you up."

But Morgan shrugged away from her hand. "I am perfectly capable of getting up."

"Are you always so stubborn?"

Morgan glared at her. "Are you always so annoying?"

Reese laughed. "Yeah. Pretty much."

"Figures."

But after three attempts to right herself, Morgan reluctantly took Reese's hand and let herself be pulled to her feet. It was at that very moment when Reese smiled smugly at her that she snapped. Quick as a cat, she shoved Reese as hard as she could, sending her toppling over into a snowdrift. She grinned wickedly, then wobbled again, her skis pointing in opposite directions as her legs spread apart, doing the split. *Oh, crap.*

And down she went.

Reese's laughter echoed in the forest, sending her into another fit of annoyance. But as she sat in the snow, she realized the absurdity of the situation—two grown women acting like children. She let her own laughter bubble out and fell back, staring at the blue sky overhead.

"Again, I don't think I like you very much."

"Yeah, I know." Reese sat up. "Not many people do."

Morgan leaned up again and brushed the snow off her jacket. She watched the smile fade from Reese's face. "What's your real name?"

"Hmm?"

"Your name? I don't see a mother naming her baby girl Reese. Is it short for something?"

"Now, if I told you that, I'd lose my *Zula* advantage."

"This is true. But I can't imagine it being anywhere near as hideous."

"No, no. It's not hideous. In fact, my mother tried her best to make me into a little Clarice—dance lessons, piano, ballet," she said, making a face. "Very stressful time in my life."

"Clarice, huh? Nice."

Reese got to her feet easily, then offered her hand to help Morgan up. "My older brother started calling me Reese first. My mother gave up on me being her little ballerina when I was twelve."

Morgan took her hand and stood, holding it for a second as she regained her balance. "Just the one brother?"

"No. I have a younger brother too." Reese pushed off. "Is this where you start asking about family and such?"

Morgan followed, pushing her skis into the rut that Reese had created. "Isn't that what you do when you meet someone new? Isn't that how you get to know them?"

"Do you want to get to know me?"

"Hey, you're the one who started this."

Reese stopped. "It's really pretty up here. What trail is this again?"

"Cutter's Ridge. Up at the point of the ridge, there's a trail that goes down the mountain to a stream. It's very steep and I've never tried it. It's got some deep pools in it that seldom get fished. Ed Wade says the biggest cutthroat trout he's ever caught came from there."

"He's the fishing guide?"

"Yeah. He's born and raised around here. I'd guess he knows every stream, creek and river in the county."

"I've heard his name. But I don't fish."

Like a shadow crossing the sun, Reese's expression changed from friendly to distant again. Just like that. She pushed on, following Reese up the trail—laboring was more like it. Despite the colder temperatures up this high, she could feel the perspiration on her skin from their excursion. And excursion it was as she was too involved with staying upright to enjoy the pristine freshness of the snow. She finally stopped, her breath again coming fast, frosting around her.

"Break?"

Morgan nodded. "Have I mentioned I hate cross-country skiing?"

"A couple of times, yeah."

Morgan studied her, wondering at the serious look on her face. "Where are you from?"

"Winter Park."

Morgan shook her head. "No. You know, where's your family? Your brothers." She saw Reese sigh, saw her look away. So, not a favorite subject, obviously.

"I'm from the Vegas area," she finally answered. "Stayed there after college. I was a cop on the streets for nearly ten years."

"Tired of the desert, huh?"

"Tired of the heat, the drugs, the crime, yeah, tired of the desert."

"Do you get back much? I mean, is your family still there?"

Reese gave a half-smile. "Full of questions today, Zula?"

Morgan refused to be baited. "Just making conversation, that's all." She pushed off with her poles, skiing closer. "Besides, the whole town is curious about you. Maybe I'm fishing for information."

Reese laughed. "I can assure you, other than the mayor's wife and that whole ordeal, there aren't any lurid secrets in my closet."

Morgan stared at her. "I don't believe you." Then she smiled. "But you can keep your secrets for now." She skied past her, thankful the trail took a downward turn. Of course, for every down slope there was another climb. She could already feel her muscles protesting. Not that she didn't get a fair amount of exercise during the summer. She was out on the trails often. But the colder it got, the more she found she enjoyed her forest patrols from the comfort of her truck. And of course, once the snows came, hiking was out of the question. But she knew she would suffer tomorrow as her hamstrings and quads tightened up.

She let her momentum carry her up the next hill, then slipped into the sliding steps that propelled her up the trail. At the top, she rested, waiting on Reese to climb the hill. She took a deep breath, enjoying the fragrance of the spruce trees. There was a subtle difference in the smells between winter and summer. Maybe it was the snow that made it seem fresher in the winter, but there was a cleanness to the air that you didn't find in summer.

"You're better than you let on," Reese said. "You have a natural fluid movement."

"Which doesn't serve me well when I fall down."

"It's an art to getting back up."

"So I've been told."

"Maybe you should just work on not—"

Before the rifle shot even registered with her, Reese had taken her to the ground, covering her body with her own.

"What the hell are you doing?"

"I suppose you didn't hear the rifle shot?"

"Yes, I heard it." Morgan tried to push her off and shifted, only to have Reese slip between her legs. Their eyes met and Morgan gasped. "What the hell is that?"

"It's my weapon. Did you think I grew a penis overnight or something?" She rolled off her. "Stay down."

Morgan watched as she unsnapped her boots from the skis, then slid down the trail. She shook her head, then sat up, unsnapping her own boots.

"What the hell are you doing? Are you trying to get killed? I said stay the hell down."

"Oh, good Lord," Morgan muttered as she stood, looking up the mountain where the shot came from. "Johnnie!" she yelled. She saw him step from behind the trees not too far up the mountain, holding his rifle steady. "Jesus Christ, Johnnie! What the hell's the matter with you? You could have shot us." She turned, finding Reese holding her gun, pointing it at Johnnie. "Lower your weapon, Chief. He's harmless."

"I don't think so. Him first."

Morgan held up her hands. "Johnnie? What the hell?"

"I wasn't trying to shoot you. If I was, you'd be dead."

"Then what the hell?"

He walked closer, pausing to spit tobacco juice, spoiling the white snow. "Damn trespassers, that's what. They come out here on their damn snowmobiles, their damn skis. I'm sick of it. And that no-good lady sheriff won't even take my calls."

Morgan smiled and turned to Reese, eyebrows raised. "Any comment?"

Reese lowered her gun. "You want to put that rifle down, sir?"

He squinted. "Who the hell are you?"

Morgan laughed. "Johnnie, this is the no-good lady sheriff, Reese Daniels."

Johnnie studied her. "Damn, she's pretty."

Morgan stared at Reese, a smile playing on her lips. "Kinda, yeah. But she's a little arrogant. Definitely moody."

"Most women are."

Reese stepped forward. "Excuse me, but lower your goddamn rifle."

"Impatient too," Morgan added.

Johnnie finally slung his rifle over his shoulder and offered his hand. "I'm Johnnie Cutter."

"Ah. Cutter's Ridge."

He nodded. "This trail skirts the ridge. My property is on up the mountain and down the other side. And as I was saying, those damn tourists think they own the whole goddamn mountain. And I want some action."

"Have you posted signs?"

Johnnie snorted. "Tell her, Morgan."

"They come up the canyon from the trail on snowmobiles. At the top of the canyon is an avalanche chute. It's got deep snow at an awesome angle," she said. "It's like skiing a black diamond."

"And it's on my property."

"I see." Reese looked at Morgan. "And what does the Forest Service plan to do about it?"

Morgan shrugged. "We've put up signs, danger warnings, avalanche warnings. Nothing deters them. And as you know, it's just me and Charlie this time of year."

"And so you want *my* staff to do something? Googan?" She laughed. "Although it would be fun seeing him give chase on a snowmobile."

"I've asked Rick Patterson to post signs at his place, but he says that's what most of the thrill riders come up here for. Cutter's Chute."

"Well, we'll have to work on a plan then." She turned to Johnnie. "And, Mr. Cutter, if I hear of you firing your rifle at tourists, I'll have your ass in jail so fast you won't know what hit you." She smiled. "Clear?"

He scratched his stubbly beard then spit tobacco juice into the snow again. "I just think I have a right to—"

"Spare me the trespassing bullshit. My guess is that Cutter's Chute is nowhere near your house, but it just pisses you off that tourists *dare* leave the forest and go on private land. We'll do what we can to stop them, but obviously we can't post a sentry here to guard it. But I'll file attempted murder charges on you right now for shooting at us if you don't mind my words."

"Attempted murder? Morgan, tell her. Hell, I learned how to handle a gun when I was eight years old. There ain't no *attempted murder* here."

Reese pointed her finger at him. "No more shooting at the tourists."

Morgan stepped forward. "Johnnie, we'll work out something. Might not be until summer. Maybe we can put up a fence or something down in the canyon to cut off their route. How's that?"

"Summer ain't going to help me this winter now, is it?"

"I'll take a snowmobile out myself. I'll see what I can do," Morgan promised. "But, Johnnie, you can't go trying to scare people off with your rifle."

"Man's got a right to protect his property."

Morgan smiled and squeezed his arm. "I know, Johnnie. But you've got to stop worrying about it so much. People are gonna do what they're going to do."

He nodded. "Yeah, they do, don't they?" He turned to Reese. "Nice to meet you. Maybe you'll take my calls now instead of having that nosy Eloise put me off. It's not like I call for the fun of it, you know. Hell, I've got to hike a half-mile up the ridge just to get a signal on that fancy cell phone I got. The least you could do is take my call."

"Of course."

He gave them both a curt nod and disappeared back into the forest. Morgan grabbed Reese's arm as she turned.

"He doesn't do it just because he's an ornery old man. His grandson died on Cutter's Chute about ten years ago. His only grandchild. So whining about the tourists is just an excuse. He doesn't want anyone else to lose their life to it."

"I see. Is it that dangerous?"

"If you don't know what you're doing, yeah. I'd say since I've been here, five or six have flipped their machines flying down the chute. Broken legs, broken back. Had one we had to airlift out by helicopter."

Reese watched her. "You been out on it?"

Morgan shook her head. "No. I mean, I love to ride fast, but I'm not that skilled." She grinned. "Or that crazy."

CHAPTER SIXTEEN

"Old Johnnie shot at you?" Charlie laughed. "I bet finding out she was the sheriff 'bout made him swallow his tobacco."

"Especially when Reese threatened to haul him in for attempted murder."

Charlie watched her. "Reese, huh?"

Morgan shrugged. "That's her name. I'm not going to go around calling her 'Chief.'"

"So, you like her okay? You didn't push her off the mountain?"

Morgan laughed. "I came close. But yeah, she lightened up some. But she's still going to need some work."

"Well, good. Maybe you can—"

"No, Charlie. Not you too." She leaned across his desk and met his eyes. "Do *not* try to play matchmaker."

"No, I don't think you'd go together. You're too independent, too strong-willed. I think you would clash with her seeing as how I'd describe her the same way."

"Uh-huh." Morgan straightened up. She didn't believe him

for a second. "Don't you dare repeat this, but it was actually kinda fun."

"Maybe the only reason you hate skiing is because you've never had a good partner before."

"Trust me, that ain't it." She sighed. "I'm calling it a day. I think I'll go over to Sloan's for a beer. Want to come?"

"I may come over later. I just got started on the damn budget for next season. They want to cut our funding again and I've got to prove why we need it." He shook his head. "Damn politicians stick money in all these useless projects and leave us hanging out to dry. What do they think? That three people can manage a million acres of forest land?"

"Oh, we'll manage, Charlie, we always do."

"Yeah, well once you get your truck back, you better hope it doesn't die on you because I'm not budgeting for repairs."

"Right." She smiled on her way out. He said that every year. In fact, sure as she'd bitch about winter, he'd bitch about the upcoming budget. Same thing every year from both of them. It dawned on her then that this would be the last time they'd have that particular conversation. Charlie's last season. It wouldn't be the same around here, that's for sure. Her only hope was that they wouldn't bring in someone so opposite of Charlie that she couldn't stand to work for them. After seven years—eight by that time—this was home. She'd hate to request a transfer this late in her career. She'd been working for the Service fourteen years. Sixteen more and she'd be eligible to retire. Not that her retirement could sustain her, but at least she'd have a nice nest egg, something to fall back on if she wanted to start something new, or maybe just go to part-time.

Thirty-five and thinking about retirement. How sad.

Reese was going to skip her usual meal at Sloan's. She was tired from skiing and wanted nothing more than to soak in a tub of hot water and relax. Unfortunately, her culinary skills were nonexistent. And she knew for a fact there was nothing in her pantry or fridge. She had the last piece of stale bread for her breakfast toast that morning.

So she pulled in front of Sloan's Bar, pleased to see Morgan's rented Jeep parked nearby. All in all, their outing had been pleasant, if you didn't mind a rifle being shot over your head. Which normally she did, she thought with a smile. If Morgan was alone at the bar, she might just opt to sit up there by her instead of by herself at a booth. It'd give them another opportunity to get to know each other.

She slammed her truck door, knowing that was just an excuse. Truth was, she was a little intrigued by Morgan. The woman was full of questions but had divulged little about her own life. There had to be a reason she stayed in Lake City. And as far as she could tell, Morgan was very single, so it wasn't a woman who kept her here. Because frankly, she couldn't imagine *anyone* staying in this tiny town willingly. No, when her year was up, she'd be gone the next day.

Morgan was where she thought she'd be—sitting at the bar chatting with Tracy. She walked over casually, ignoring the stares of the other patrons. Those who knew her routine knew she never went to the bar.

"Evening, ladies," she said as she sat on the high-backed barstool beside Morgan.

Morgan smiled easily at her. "You're able to walk?"

Reese laughed. "So far. Tomorrow might be another story."

"Excuse me, Chief Daniels, but did you want your usual?"

"Tracy, you know it's okay to call me Reese." She glanced at Morgan, noting her amused expression at Tracy's formality. Then again, Tracy was probably in shock that Reese could speak in complete sentences. "And Eloise tells me I need to try the double battered chicken. What do you think?"

"Oh, yes, ma'am, it's delicious. Comes with a side salad and some steak fries."

"Sounds great. And I'll have a beer while I'm waiting." She turned in her barstool and met Morgan's eyes, giving her a subtle wink as Tracy hurried to fill a mug.

78

"A month of burgers is enough for you?"

Reese shrugged. "When you don't cook, it's hard to be choosy. Especially in this town."

"I've found that when people say they don't cook, it means they don't *like* to cook, not that they can't."

Reese nodded at Tracy who disappeared after sliding a beer in front of her. "I suppose you cook?"

Morgan laughed. "Not really, no. I mean, I wouldn't starve to death or anything. Actually, I know how to cook. I just hate doing it."

Reese sipped from her beer, watching Morgan do the same. "Why are you here?"

Morgan raised her eyebrows. "Here?"

"In Lake City," she clarified. "I mean, you asked me that question once."

"Oh, I see. You view it as being stuck here. And I guess maybe that first winter, I did too. I was supposed to be assigned to Gunnison and Blue Mesa. But on the very day I got there, they said I'd been transferred. And when I saw this town and realized how remote it would be, especially during the winter, I panicked. I was going to transfer out the next season."

"Yet here you are."

"Yeah. I fell in love with the place, the people. So I thought, well, I'll do another year, then transfer out." She laughed. "Seven years ago."

"Don't you miss having a relationship?"

"You mean sex? Don't I miss having sex?"

Reese smiled. "Yeah."

"Of course. Why do you think I let Moaning Mona come home with me?"

Reese coughed and nearly spit her beer out. "*Moaning Mona?*"

"Sorry."

Reese shook her head. "I don't want to know."

"But I told you she was a biter, right?"

"No. Again, I don't want to know."

Morgan laughed. "You see, this is why it's nice to have another lesbian in town. I can't talk about my sex life—or lack of—with the girls. Tracy wants to lecture me about settling down and Tina just wants more details."

"So we're really the only two around, huh?"

"No. Actually, there's a couple that live up the mountain, past Charlie's place. But they're either very closeted or they live like hermits intentionally. They're pretty self-sufficient, from what I hear. They have a big greenhouse to grow vegetables and they have solar panels for their power. They come into town some during the summer, but winter, no, we don't see them until spring thaw."

"How long have they been here?"

"They came the year after me. So six years."

Reese rested her elbows on the bar, nodding at Tracy to refill her mug. "So again, why are you here?"

"Are you saying I should base my whole existence on the possibility of romance? I have little shot of it here, so I should move?" Morgan shrugged. "If I were younger, maybe. But I'll turn thirty-six this spring, I love it here, I love the people, I'm content with my life. I don't want to move somewhere just to increase my chances of meeting someone I might possibly have a relationship with. I guess what I'm saying is, at this point in my life, it's not that big a deal, as long as I'm happy with everything else." She paused. "And I am."

"And you get by with the occasional dalliance with someone like Mona?"

Morgan laughed again, an easy laugh that Reese found enjoyable.

"Dalliance? Is that what it was?" Morgan leaned closer and playfully bumped her arm. "Is that what *you* called it? You and the mayor's wife?"

"Even though Winter Park is a hell of a lot more glamorous than Lake City, it wasn't exactly crawling with single gay women."

"I'm assuming the mayor's wife is straight?"

Reese smiled. "Oh, yes. Very straight. And I'm afraid I ruined it for her."

"Rocked her world, did you?"

"She's fifty-one and had never had oral sex."

"Oh, my."

"Yeah, it was quite fun." Not enough fun to get booted out of town though. She looked up as Tracy placed her bag on the bar. "Thanks, Tracy."

"Or did you want to eat here tonight, Chief?"

"No. I should get going." She glanced at Morgan. "What are you having?"

"Oh, I'll probably get a burger to take home." She slid her beer mug over to Tracy. "But I'll have one more."

Reese took her bag and moved the barstool back, then tossed a ten-dollar bill on the bar. "Beer's on me, Zula," she teased quietly, barely moving fast enough to miss the punch Morgan threw at her.

"I will so kill you."

"Now, now. Don't cause a scene." Reese bowed politely. "Goodnight, Morgan. See you around." She nodded at Tracy before escaping out the door, realizing that she was still smiling. Yeah, she liked Morgan. It'd be nice to have someone to talk to, a friend.

But later, as she sat alone at her table in her quiet little cabin, finishing off the last of the steak fries, she wondered if she could go the whole year with Morgan as a friend. Truth was, she found her attractive. They had easy conversations. Nothing was ever strained or forced. But she couldn't actually see herself asking Morgan out on a date. For one thing, what would they do? Where would they go? Sloan's Bar was the only entertainment in the county.

"Forget it," she murmured, gathering the remains of her dinner and tossing it in the trash.

She went into the living room, bored out of her mind, knowing it was too early for bed. She turned a circle, looking around the small cabin. When she'd agreed to take this job, it was one of the things she insisted on—a place to live that wasn't in town. And a place she didn't have to pay for.

They came up with this little jewel. It belonged to Ronald Brightmen, one of the county commissioners. It was a vacation and hunting cabin that seldom got used, he'd told her. And it suited her perfectly. Six miles out of town, at the edge of the National Forest, no nosy neighbors and absolutely no traffic.

And she was bored and lonely and starting to think crazy thoughts.

Like wondering if Morgan was as feisty *in* bed as she was out of it.

CHAPTER SEVENTEEN

Morgan glanced up as the door opened, smiling when Tina stuck her head inside.

"Hey, guys," she said as she came in carrying a picnic basket. "I brought lunch."

"Bored, are you?"

"Totally." Tina plopped down beside Morgan's desk and winked at Berta. "Besides, I've been hearing all sorts of rumors. I came to check them out."

Morgan eyed Berta suspiciously. "What kind of rumors?"

"You and Chief Daniels spending time together."

Morgan rolled her eyes. "Good grief. We went skiing."

"That in itself is big news. You hate to ski."

"Yes, I know. Charlie made me."

"And dinner?"

"Dinner? We didn't have dinner."

"My source tells me you were seen at Sloan's together."

"I know your source is Tracy, and she knows perfectly well that Reese just stopped by and chatted while she was waiting for her dinner."

"Reese? That's kind of familiar, isn't it?"

"Tina, quit trying to read something into it." She pointed her finger at her. "And *do not* try to play matchmaker." Morgan looked at Berta. "And you, I know you're the one who told her about skiing. And you know very well I didn't want to do it."

"I don't know what you're talking about," Berta said as she stood. "But it is lunchtime. I'm meeting Eloise at the café."

"I swear, I can't take a crap without half the town knowing about it," she said when Berta closed the door.

Tina laughed. "It's winter. There's nothing going on. Your love life gets top billing, I'm afraid."

"Love life? I don't have a love life."

"Not yet, no, but we're working on it."

"Seriously, you have got to stop it. So we went skiing. No big deal. So we saw each other at Sloan's. Again, not unusual. She eats there nearly every night. It wasn't like it was a *date* or anything." She pulled the basket closer. "What'd you bring, anyway?"

"Venison stew."

Morgan grinned. "How sweet. My favorite." She pulled out the two covered bowls and placed them on her desk, then put the basket aside. "I love when you bring me your leftovers."

"You can't make just a little when you're making stew or soup. Besides, you know how my kids are when it comes to leftovers."

"Yes. That's one thing I miss when you don't work during the winter, I don't eat as well."

"Speaking of eating, you're going to be on your own for Christmas this year," Tina said as she pulled the top off each bowl and handed Morgan a spoon. "Paul's mother is renting a beach house in South Florida for the holidays. She said she refuses to have everyone traveling in the snow, just so we can get together."

"The beach? That's not Christmas," Morgan said. She took a bite and groaned. "This is so good."

"Thanks. And I know. We'll be building snowmen out of sand."

"But I guess it'll be a good break. The kids will love the beach."

"I just wish she would have consulted everyone instead of just doing it. It's so like her, just thinking of herself."

"Oh, you'll have a good time," she said. "You know, I'm from Florida. You just get used to Christmas being warm. It was no big deal."

"And I'm from Colorado and you get used to there being snow at Christmas," Tina replied, sticking her tongue out at Morgan. "Don't try to pacify me. I'm allowed to be pissed at my mother-in-law if I want to be."

Morgan grinned. "Sorry. I didn't realize it was the control factor going on here. I thought you were just upset you were going to the beach." She waved her spoon in the air. "Of course, you have every right to be pissed at her for arranging such a horrible, horrible trip."

"Oh, shut up. See if I bring you lunch anymore."

Morgan pulled out the bottom drawer of her desk, then leaned back in her chair and propped her feet on top of the drawer, balancing her bowl on her stomach. This was something she missed when Tina got laid off for winter, her bringing in leftovers for lunch. "You know, it wouldn't hurt for you to come around more. Just because you're not working, we could still pop over to Sloan's for lunch occasionally."

"I know. But I'm trying to be the productive stay-at-home mom. House is clean, laundry is done, and dinner is on the table when the hubby and kids get home."

"How boring. And do you polish the silverware and dust all of the shelves?"

"It does sound boring, doesn't it? And don't cringe, but I've started watching soaps again."

"This is the year you *swore* you weren't going to get hooked on them again," Morgan reminded her.

"Well, if *you* had a love life to talk about, perhaps I wouldn't have to."

Morgan smiled sweetly. "Enjoy your soaps, then. After the last encounter with Moaning Mona, I think it's safer to remain celibate."

Celibate, yes, but that didn't mean she couldn't look. Because Reese Daniels was far too attractive to just skim over.

"Okay, so you're here first the other night and she comes in and joins you at the bar," Tracy said as she filled a mug for her. "Tonight, she's here first, sitting at her usual booth, and you come in and totally ignore her." She slid the beer toward her. "What's up with that?"

"Nothing's up. But if I go over there and talk to her, then you'll tell Tina and she'll tell Berta. Then half the town will think something's going on with us. Which it's not."

Tracy laughed. "Like I didn't just see you checking her out."

"I was not."

"Was too."

Morgan felt her face flush. "Okay, so I never said she wasn't attractive or anything. She is. She's just not my type."

"Oh, quit being so stubborn and go talk to her. I'll stall her dinner."

Morgan sighed. "Again, what's with you straight women trying to set me up? Am I that pathetic that you all feel sorry for me?" Morgan narrowed her eyes. "And why doesn't anyone try to set you up?"

"Oh, please. Who would they set me up with?"

"Maybe you should go off to college then."

"That's not something you tell someone who is about to turn thirty." Tracy leaned closer. "Besides, the only eligible guys around here are the seasonal cowboys who work Thompson's Ranch." She shook her head. "And I'm just not interested." She motioned again to Reese Daniels. "But she's cute. You should go talk to her."

"Good grief." Morgan got up and took her beer. "Okay,

I'll go talk to her." As she walked across the bar, even though conversations went on around her, she felt eyes on her as she approached Reese's table.

"She finally talked you into coming over, huh?" Reese said without taking her eyes off the magazine she'd been reading.

"She's trying to play matchmaker, I'm afraid." Morgan slid into the booth opposite her. "Along with Tina. I'm fairly certain it's a conspiracy."

Reese's eyebrows shot up. "With me?"

"Of course with you."

"Who's Tina again?"

"She works with me. Seasonal. She and her husband are good friends of mine."

"I see." She tossed the magazine aside and folded her hands together. "And what do you think about this...this *matchmaking*?"

Morgan laughed. "I told them you weren't my type."

"That's right. I'm *brooding* or something. Isn't that what you said?"

Morgan spun her mug between her hands. "Actually, you thought I wanted to sleep with you and you politely said you weren't interested."

Reese looked across the table and met her eyes. "Speaking of that, perhaps we should revisit that conversation."

"What do you mean?"

"I mean, maybe we should reconsider."

Morgan's eyes widened. "Reconsider *sleeping* together? Are you serious?"

Reese shrugged. "Why not?"

"For one, you weren't interested, remember?"

"I'm not interested in dating anyone, no."

Morgan studied her. "And why is that? Not that I want to date you either," Morgan quickly clarified.

"Dating leads to being a couple. That leads to living together."

"Have a problem with monogamy, do you?"

"No, no. That's not it. It's just a big cycle is all. You live together a few years, you grow bored, you split up, you start all over with someone else and do the same thing. I just don't see the point."

"That's crazy. The point is, if you fall in love with someone, you want to be with them, which means living together."

"Yes, well, I'm not interested in that."

"But you are interested in sex?"

Reese smiled. "I like you. I think you like me. We're both of age and single."

"So...so you want to have sex...with *me*?"

"It's the middle of winter and I'm thinking we're both bored out of our minds already. I know I am. What harm would there be for us to get together on a cold night and release a little pent-up energy? No strings. Just a physical, sexual relationship."

Morgan stared at her, stunned by her words. "And you're serious?"

"Look, if the idea of sleeping with me is disgusting, just say so. I mean, we're friends. Or we're becoming friends. So if you think we can't *still* be friends—"

"With sex on the side?"

"Yeah."

"Oh, my God! I can't believe we're having this conversation. I've *never* done anything like that before."

"Yet you have sex with a perfect stranger?"

"I was drunk. And lonely." She leaned forward. "So would this be like a once a week thing or what?"

Reese picked up her soggy paper coaster and twirled it between her fingers. "I don't know. Whenever we like, I guess."

Morgan grinned. "So, do we have a secret sign? You know, to let the other one know?"

"So now you're making fun?"

"No. I'm just shocked that I'm actually considering this. Because you know, I'm not certain I even like you."

"Now that's not true."

"No, it's not, I guess. I haven't thrown my beer in your face yet because of this proposition."

Reese leaned closer, her voice low. "Look, if we try it and find it's not going to work, then no one has to know. We'll just go about our business. If it's enjoyable to both of us, then what's the harm? I'm here eleven more months then I'm gone. And frankly, the thought of spending eleven months without female company is not all that appealing."

"Tell me, Chief Daniels, do you make these kinds of propositions often?"

Reese looked up as Jeff brought over her dinner. "Thanks, Jeff."

"Sure thing. Can I get you anything else? Morgan?"

"I'll need another beer, Jeff." Or perhaps she should switch to something stronger. *A no strings affair with Reese Daniels*? Good Lord...

Reese stood and placed her money under the empty beer mug. "And no, I've never made this type of proposition to anyone. I've never been in exile before."

Morgan watched her walk away, her eyes lingering on her backside. *Oh, my.* Dare she agree to this? To this *crazy* plan? It was a long, cold winter, she reasoned. And there was no Jackson at home to keep her company. Perhaps Reese was on to something. What harm could it be?

She shook her head. Surely to God she wasn't seriously considering this? Was she that lonely, that starved for physical contact that she would consider having sex with Reese Daniels just for fun? No commitment. No attachments. Hell, no rules. Just sex. Sex for the sake of having sex.

She thought she should be embarrassed—or better yet, disgusted—by the proposition. But she wasn't. Because, yeah, Reese Daniels wasn't really her type, no. But she was cute, attractive, and Morgan could just imagine what her body would look like naked.

Oh, my.

"Hey."

She jumped, startled, as Tracy held her fresh beer out to her.

"Gonna come back to the bar or sit here?"

She stared dumbly at her. Should she tell her? *Good grief, no!* So she nodded. "At the bar."

"You okay?"

"Yeah, I'm fine. Why?"

"You look a little pale. Did the Chief upset you or something?"

"Or something," Morgan murmured as she followed Tracy back to the bar.

CHAPTER EIGHTEEN

Reese stared out the window into the darkness, listening absently as the coffee slowly dripped into the pot, spewing steam from the top occasionally. The restlessness she'd been feeling for the last couple of weeks had not diminished and here she was, staring out at the deserted street, the lone light flickering over Sloan's Bar, not even a hint of the morning sun to penetrate the darkness.

She shook her head, wondering what had possessed her to make such a preposterous proposal to Morgan last night. Was she that *lonely*? That *desperate* for female company that she'd proposition the only other lesbian in town?

"Apparently."

Of course the fact that Morgan hadn't tossed her beer in her face—or worse, slapped her—was a bit intriguing. Was Morgan actually considering it?

Reese let out a sigh, wondering what her reaction would be should Morgan show up on her doorstep, fully prepared to accept the proposition. What would she do?

She turned away from the window, heading toward the smell of the freshly brewed coffee. Oh, she knew exactly what she'd do. Morgan was attractive and she stirred enough sexual interest to make a physical relationship appealing. She assumed the same was true for Morgan.

It was just cold enough this morning to be uncomfortable and Morgan turned the heat up just a little in the truck. Truth was, she was glad to get it back. As much fun as she had in the Jeep, it wasn't airtight by any means, and she had a heck of a time getting warm. The Forest Service uniforms were not meant for winter, and she could only layer so much beneath the cotton shirt. Of course, they weren't meant for summer either and she ended up sweltering in the drab green cotton. Charlie had gotten used to her breaking the uniform code though—jeans in the winter and shorts in summer. Except when his bosses paid a visit, then she dutifully donned the drab green cotton pants that matched the drab green shirt.

And why she was going over her wardrobe so early this morning wasn't as perplexing to her as she'd hoped. But it filled her mind with trivial dribble and kept her from replaying the proposition Reese Daniels had laid on the table last night.

Because frankly she'd replayed it so much, she felt like she hadn't slept at all. No, that's because instead of sleeping, she was imagining being in bed with Reese Daniels—in bed, naked and having sex.

She gripped the steering wheel, trying to push out the images that were still fresh in her mind. Several things surprised her. Mainly, that she was actually considering the proposition. And secondly, how could she possibly know what Reese Daniels looked like naked? But in her mind, certainly last night, she could vividly picture her without clothes, her brooding dark eyes seeing more than they should, her unruly hair a tousled mess after their lovemaking.

"Oh, good grief," she said as she quickly turned the heat off and cracked the window. It was crazy to even think about, much less consider *doing* it. For one thing, it would be all over town, no matter how discreet they planned to be. And did she really want the locals scrutinizing her love life? Everyone knew that Chief Daniels was here only for the one year. What would that say about Morgan if she carried on an affair with her, knowing she was leaving? Then *everyone* would know it was only for the sex!

Of course, they could do a trial run, as Reese suggested. Maybe they weren't compatible in bed. Maybe it would be awkward. Maybe there would be no sexual energy between them.

Or maybe it would be fabulous and Morgan would care less what everyone was saying. There was sex, and then there was fabulous sex.

"You have *lost* your mind," she whispered as she turned down the Alpine Loop Byway that followed Henson Creek. The loop was heavily traveled in the summer as Jeeps and four-wheel-drive trucks descended upon them, taking the scenic drive from Lake City to Silverton as the rough road hugged Engineer Mountain and Cinnamon Mountain, each view more breathtaking than the one before. Even after seven summers here, she still found time at least once each season to rent a Jeep from the Rocky Alpine Crew and take her chances with Engineer Pass at nearly thirteen thousand feet.

Her pleas to Charlie that she needed her own Jeep to patrol the Forest Service roads had failed to produce one for her.

The road was deserted this cold morning, as it would be for the rest of the winter, except for those adventurous souls who would drive to Cinnamon cutoff and cross-country ski along the ridge. Her drive here this morning was just an excuse to get out and think, really. There were no campsites to check on, no fishing licenses to validate, no warnings to be issued as people went off-road where they weren't supposed to. No tourists, no worries.

Winter loomed. A long, cold winter. A long, cold, *lonely* winter.

But it didn't have to be lonely. It didn't even have to be cold. Hot sex would alleviate both of those things.

Hot sex with Reese Daniels.

CHAPTER NINETEEN

Reese saw Morgan's truck parked at Sloan's Bar and she almost stopped. They'd not spoken in two days and she didn't want to make Morgan uncomfortable by stalking her at the bar. She'd give it a week. If nothing came of it, then she'd go back to her solitary ways, sitting at the booth by herself, waiting on her dinner that she'd eat alone at home.

But she had a feeling she wouldn't have to wait a week. They'd not spoken, but Reese had seen Morgan on the street as she and Berta passed the sheriff's office on their way to lunch today. Their eyes had met through the window, and in that brief moment, Reese saw what she'd hoped she'd see—a secret look passed between them, a look that indicated Morgan had an interest. Whether she followed through on that interest was another story.

So she drove past the bar, heading out of town, turning when she reached the unpaved road that would take her to her temporary home. She had no doubt Morgan knew where she lived even though they'd not discussed it. Like most residents of this tiny mountain town, she assumed Morgan knew pretty much everything about everybody.

Morgan twirled her beer, glancing up each time the door opened, looking for Reese. Because if Reese showed up, then that meant she wasn't at her house waiting on her…waiting for her to have sex. *Oh, my.*

"You okay?"

Morgan smiled at Tracy and nodded. "Of course."

Tracy leaned closer. "You seem nervous." She looked at the door. "The chief is thirty minutes late. Wonder if she's skipping dinner tonight."

Morgan shrugged nonchalantly.

"You want a burger?"

"No, I'm good."

Tracy moved down to the other end of the bar to wait on Doug Fender, and Morgan again slid her gaze to the door. She knew Reese wasn't coming. She knew Reese was waiting for her. She knew that from the look they'd shared today. Just a brief glance, their eyes meeting through the windowpane of the sheriff's office. But that glance said it all—Reese was waiting for her. In the few seconds that their eyes held, Morgan was ready to say *yes, yes, yes* to her proposition. In fact, if Berta hadn't been with her, she might have gone inside to tell Reese *yes* right then. But the moment passed, and she and Berta walked on to the café, Berta none the wiser to the look between them.

So now what? Reese was waiting and here she sat, nursing a beer that had gone warm, ignoring Tracy and everyone else in the bar, trying to calm her nerves and find the courage to do what she wanted to do.

Go to Reese Daniels.

Reese had just put another log on the fire when she heard the truck door slam. She cocked her head, her gut telling her Morgan was about to knock on her door. And her nerves told her she wasn't certain she was ready for it. She looked around the room, the lamp in the corner casting the only light other than the dancing flames of the fire.

After the quick—quiet—tap on her door, she took a deep breath, then opened it. Morgan stood there, her eyes shifting about nervously. Reese offered a small smile, hoping it would calm Morgan. And herself.

"I have two rules," Morgan said.

Reese nodded. "Okay."

"I want to keep this as discreet as possible and…and no kissing."

Reese raised an eyebrow. "Don't like kissing?"

"No, no, that's not it. I love kissing. To me, kissing is the most romantic, personal—intimate—thing you can do."

"Okay. And?"

"And to keep this…this thing," she said, pointing between them, "to keep it as a physical, sexual act only, I don't think kissing should be allowed."

"I see."

Reese took Morgan's hand and pulled her across the threshold, shutting the door behind her. Morgan's hand was warm and she squeezed it, standing close to her, using the door to prevent Morgan's escape.

"I can live with your rules," she said, her voice low. "I'm assuming you mean kissing on the lips only." She moved closer, watching as Morgan swallowed nervously. She moved her mouth to Morgan's ear. "You don't have a problem if I kiss you here, right?" She felt Morgan's breath catch. "Or here?" she whispered as her lips moved against Morgan's neck. She smelled clean and fresh and Reese let her lips linger.

"Oh, *God*," Morgan whispered before her hands slid up Reese's arms.

No other words were spoken. Morgan leaned back, offering

herself. Reese shoved Morgan's sweater up then tugged at the undershirt beneath it, pulling it from Morgan's jeans, her lips still nibbling gently at Morgan's neck.

Her first touch of warm flesh sent her senses reeling. Her hands glided across Morgan's skin, resting just below her breasts. She lifted her head, finding Morgan's eyes, her breathing as rapid as Morgan's as the soft sounds filled the cabin.

"Okay?" she whispered.

Morgan's eyes slipped closed. "Yes."

Yes. She cupped Morgan's full breasts, impatiently shoving her bra aside, letting them fill her hands. She felt the hard nipples cut into her palms and she moaned, wanting her mouth there. Without thinking, she pulled Morgan's sweater and undershirt over her head, then nearly ripped her bra as she unclasped it and let it fall to the floor.

"Beautiful," she whispered as her mouth found one of Morgan's breasts. She felt Morgan's hands thread through her hair, holding her close, moaning softly as Reese teased her nipple with her tongue.

How they made it to the rug, Reese had no idea, but while her mouth feasted, her fingers deftly unbuttoned Morgan's jeans and lowered the zipper. Morgan helped her push the offending material aside, impatiently kicking the jeans off her legs.

Reese lifted her head, meeting Morgan's eyes in the soft glow of the firelight, her naked body shimmering with heat. A naked body she was about to make love to. She looked for any hint of uncertainty in Morgan's eyes and found none. Her eyes were glistening with arousal, her mouth slightly parted, her breasts rising and falling with each quick breath she took.

Letting her lips kiss and nuzzle Morgan's warm flesh, Reese moved down her body, relishing the taste of Morgan's skin. A gentle hand still rested on her head, fingers still threaded in her hair, urging her downward. The quiet moans that Morgan uttered, the subtle shifting of her hips, the rapid breathing—Reese wanted to hurry, wanting to give Morgan what she so obviously desired. But she took her time, teasing Morgan's skin with her tongue, running her hands down her legs and then up again, feeling the wetness between her thighs.

"Reese, *please*," she whispered as Reese kissed inside her thigh, still teasing her.

The musky aroma nearly made her head spin and she parted Morgan's thighs, cupping her hips, groaning with pleasure as her mouth settled over her, tasting her for the first time. She held on tightly as Morgan's hips rose, moving slowly against her mouth, the fingers in her hair clasping and unclasping as Reese suckled her swollen clit.

"Oh, God *yes*," Morgan breathed. "Yes, *yes*."

As Morgan's orgasm threatened, Reese shifted, thrusting two fingers deep inside her as her tongue flicked across her clit, faster and faster, loving the sounds Morgan was making, feeling her tighten against her fingers. Morgan's hips rose off the floor and she screamed out, jerking wildly against Reese's face before slowly sinking back to the floor again.

"Dear *God*."

Reese smiled as her fingers slipped from Morgan and she rested her cheek against Morgan's thigh, listening to her rapid breathing as Morgan's hand continued to thread through her hair.

After a moment, Morgan's hand stilled and Reese heard her take a deep breath.

"I don't have one stitch of clothes on," she murmured.

Reese turned. "I see that."

"How did that happen?"

"You don't remember? Shall I show you again?"

Morgan laughed quietly. "No, no. I'm good." She leaned up on an elbow. "But perhaps you could lose the sweatshirt?"

"Just the sweatshirt?"

"For now."

Reese sat up and obliged, tossing her shirt on top of Morgan's discarded jeans.

"Oh, my," Morgan whispered.

Reese waited, watching Morgan's gaze travel across her bare

breasts. She nearly trembled when Morgan lowered her head, when she felt Morgan's warm breath caress her nipples, when she felt the first tentative touch of Morgan's tongue.

Then she was pushed back to the rug and Morgan's fingers attacked the button on her jeans.

"Naked," she murmured against her breast. "I want you naked."

And again, Reese obliged.

CHAPTER TWENTY

Reese caught herself whistling as she walked into her office. The strange look Eloise gave her made her stop immediately. Who would have known that a night of sex—really *great* sex—could put her in such a joyous mood?

"Running late today, Chief?"

Reese glanced up at the large clock hanging on the wall above Eloise's desk. "It's not even eight. Besides, I wasn't aware I had set hours, Eloise."

"It's just I haven't had to make coffee in nearly two months now, what with you beating me in every morning. I was surprised to find the place empty this morning. I thought maybe something had happened to you."

"Well, I hope you didn't do the happy dance, 'cause I'm still here." She bypassed her door and went for coffee instead. "You'll get Googan as your boss sooner or later," she added.

Eloise mumbled something too low for Reese to hear and

she smiled as she went into her office. Yes, it was going to be a great day. She spun her chair to face the small window as her computer booted up. The sun was bright, the sky cloudless, the air crisp and clean. A beautiful day. In fact, the nicest morning she could remember since she'd been in Lake City.

"Oh, Reese, a roll in the hay sure has you in a good mood," she said quietly. She wondered if Morgan's day had started out the same. Despite it being their first time together, they'd made it a memorable one. Even with Morgan's no kissing rule, they'd managed just fine, and she was exhausted when Morgan had left around midnight. Tired—and oh so sated—she fell asleep instantly, not to wake until after seven this morning. Her last sexual encounter, that with the mayor's wife, paled in comparison to what she'd shared with Morgan. One thing was for certain, they were totally compatible in bed.

Unfortunately, they'd not made plans for a second get-together. Which meant she'd be waiting again until Morgan was ready.

Morgan felt Berta's eyes on her and she was hoping—praying—that her night of free love with Reese Daniels wasn't plastered on her face. Plastered and *glowing*.

She turned away, feigning interest in the paper she was reading. She picked up a pen and forced a frown to her brow, pretending to be deeply absorbed in the latest traffic report issued for their district. That is, until Charlie tapped her on the shoulder, causing her to jump.

"Do you have to sneak up on me like that? Jeez," she said, trying to cover her embarrassment.

"Surely that report can't be *that* interesting. What'd we have? Five visitors last month?"

Morgan looked at him wryly. "Six. And it's so skewed. I mean, every one of the snowmobilers at the lodge hit our trails at one time or another."

"And if they don't sign in, it's like they were never there,"

Charlie said. "But everyone's got the same problem. You think they have an accurate account up at Blue Mesa?"

"No. But it's a huge lake. They estimate their figures on the high end. Why can't they do ours?"

"Based on what? Summer campgrounds are easy and we've got decent figures. But winter? They have nothing to use but trailhead sign-ins. It's always been that way. You know that."

"I'm just saying, it's no wonder we have no budget to work with. Why can't we have Rick *make* them sign in?"

"Rick is a businessman," Charlie said. "He's not concerned with our figures, our budget, or even our rules."

"You mean Cutter's Chute?"

"Yes. He knows—like we do—that Cutter's Chute is a big draw for him. So what if it's on private property? We conveniently have a trail that skirts the ridge. And when anyone asks him how to get there, he tells them to head up the canyon."

"Okay. So how about we put up some signs that say we are going to start issuing citations for those who *don't* sign in? We could cite some safety rule or something."

Charlie smiled. "What's all the interest in our numbers, Morgan? You afraid your position is going to get cut in the winters now?"

Morgan shrugged. "You never know. When you leave, they could bring in some hard-ass. It won't take but a few weeks during the winter for him to realize there's not a whole lot going on up here."

"Oh, Morgan, quit worrying. Your job is safe." He sat on the corner of her desk and folded his hands together. "Got a call from Chief Daniels just a bit ago."

"Oh, yeah?" Morgan commented as nonchalantly as possible.

"Seems she wanted my approval before she asked you to assist her with something."

Morgan swallowed. "Uh-huh." Then her eyes widened. "Please say it's not more skiing."

He laughed. "Afraid so."

I'll kill her.

"Seeing as how you're not busy—you said so yourself—I couldn't see turning her down."

"Thanks a lot."

"She said she wanted to take up fishing. I told her Ed Wade was her man, but she said she'd rather you show her around." He smiled mischievously. "I guess you made a good impression on her the last time."

"From her comments, I gathered she hated fishing."

He shrugged. "Wouldn't know about that. She's looking at some backcountry streams though. Off the beaten path."

"Snowmobiles can get off the beaten path."

"Too noisy."

Morgan's eyebrows drew together. "You're enjoying this far too much," she said.

"Oh, it'll do you good to get out. There's nothing going on. Hell, even Berta's got to try to scare up some paperwork to keep her busy."

"Yeah, but, Charlie, *skiing*?"

He stood. "I told her you'd love to."

Reese heard the bell jingle as the sheriff's office door was opened, then closed a bit too forcefully.

"Is she in?"

Reese smiled, recognizing Morgan's voice. And by the tone of it, Charlie had just mentioned skiing.

"Yes, Morgan. I'll just see if she's busy—"

"Trust me, she's not," Morgan said and a few seconds later, she stood at Reese's door. "Skiing? Are you *trying* to piss me off?"

Grinning, Reese got up and motioned Morgan into the room, closing the door behind her. "And good morning to you too."

"It *was* a good morning."

"Now, now."

"You don't even like fishing," Morgan said.

"I never said I didn't like to fish, I said I *don't* fish. Big difference." Reese went back around her desk and sat down, waiting for Morgan to do the same.

She finally did, albeit with a huff. When their eyes met, Reese saw a softening in them and smiled, watching a matching smile show on Morgan's face.

"I should hate you."

"But you don't."

"I'm assuming you have a legitimate *reason* for a skiing and fishing excursion?"

Reese nodded. "Last night was extremely enjoyable. Don't you think?" Reese smiled as a slight blush crossed Morgan's face.

Morgan nodded. "Yes. Yes, it was."

"Good." Reese leaned back in her chair. "But knowing you, you would have debated the merits of it and taken *days* before you'd decide to see me again."

"Days, huh?"

Reese leaned forward and smiled. "I didn't want to go days."

"I see. So you'd rather torture me with a ski trip?"

"I thought it would be a good excuse to see you. And, it might satisfy one of your rules."

"What? The *no kissing while skiing* rule?"

"I was thinking more of the *discreet* rule," Reese said. "Charlie most likely told you about my request in front of Berta. Not to disappoint, you probably bemoaned the fact that you *hate* to ski. So you march over here, ignore Eloise's attempts at office protocol and barge into my office, demanding an explanation." She pointed at the phone, showing one line in use. "And no doubt Eloise and Berta are on the phone right now, trying to figure out what is going on."

Morgan stared at her, finally smiling. "Clever. So we're just going to *pretend* to go skiing and fishing then?"

Reese laughed. "No. We have to follow through with the whole thing."

Morgan frowned. "I don't quite see the benefit. If you think I'm going to suffer through hours on skis—in the cold—then go home with you, you're crazy."

"I got the impression you liked to fish."

"Sure. In the summer, standing by a stream, my truck within sight. I *love* to fish." Morgan leaned back and crossed her ankles. "And you? Why don't you fish?"

Reese looked away for a moment, thinking that her reason was really quite silly. Especially after all these years. She cleared her throat before speaking. "Fishing was always a passion of mine. In fact, we grew up fishing almost every weekend."

"Got sick of it?"

Reese shook her head. "No. That wasn't it. My father, it was his great love. Most weekends we'd take the boat out to Lake Mead and fish dawn to dusk. Even when I was in college, I'd ditch my friends to join my brothers out on the boat." She looked across the desk, meeting Morgan's eyes. "There was an accident." She swallowed. "Freak boating accident. My father died."

"Reese, I'm so sorry."

She shrugged. "Long time ago. It took me a while to get over it. My mother, well, she never recovered. We were all there. We all saw it. We hit something, a log or something, and Dad got tossed out of the boat." She took a deep breath, still finding the words hard to say. "And the boat ran over him." She looked up. "I was driving it."

"Oh, my God," Morgan whispered. She got up, moving beside the desk and squeezing Reese's hand with her own. "I'm sorry." She shook her head. "I can't imagine your grief."

Reese took comfort in Morgan's gentle touch, and she looked at their hands, their fingers entwined, remembering Morgan's touch from last night, how those hands had moved across her body, boldly touching...*demanding*. She closed her eyes, letting her fingers play with Morgan's for a second longer before looking up.

"You better move away, or our cover is blown," she said lightly.

Morgan smiled. "Sorry."

Reese cleared her throat again. "Anyway, I wanted no part of fishing after that. Truth be told, I wanted no part of my family either. My mother, well, she never said the words, but in her eyes, I could see that she blamed me."

"Oh, Reese, surely not. It was an accident."

"Yes. That was all I had to hold on to. It was an accident. An accident that tore our family apart. Our time together got less and less. Phone calls replaced visits, and I started working myself into exhaustion so that I was too numb and too tired to remember that day. And we just drifted apart. It happened so slowly, I don't think anyone noticed."

"You don't see them at all?"

"When I quit the force in Vegas, I dropped by my mother's place, just to let her know I was leaving. I was shocked. I hadn't seen her in years. I mean, she looked like my mother, but it was just a shell. Her eyes were lifeless. All around the room, there were pictures of my father, like hundreds of pictures. My mother was living her life through those pictures, while her real life just faded away. I'm not really certain she even knew I was there."

"That's very sad."

"I went to see my brothers too. They, at least, had normal lives, kids. And they look in on her from time to time." She shrugged. "And I escaped the desert heat for the high mountains. You'd be surprised at how many tourist towns have a hard time keeping law enforcement. Jobs have been pretty easy to find."

"Maybe you're not the only one dallying with the mayor's wife?" Morgan teased.

Reese laughed. "I have learned my lesson."

"I see." Morgan paused. "So, when do you want to do this little ski trip?"

"I checked the forecast. Might hit the upper thirties tomorrow. No snow."

"And that's supposed to tempt me?"

"Okay, so what if I promised you dinner after our trip?"

"Dinner?"

"At my place."

"But you can't cook."

"Yeah, that could be a problem. Sloan's does takeout, right?"

Morgan stood. "Skiing tomorrow. We'll *talk* about dinner then." She opened the door and winked. "And the next time you need a damn ski guide, don't call me! This is the last time I'm doing this for you," she said loudly, then slammed the door behind her.

Reese hid her smile just in time as Eloise poked her head in. "Are you okay, Chief? Morgan seemed really upset."

"Apparently, she *really* hates skiing."

"I told you that the first time you had her take you out. Whatever possessed you to ask her again?"

"I think that's why she's upset. I didn't ask her. I asked Charlie." She smiled. "You know, from one official to another. We're both branches of the government, so to speak."

Eloise looked around suspiciously, then lowered her voice. "I shouldn't gossip, but Berta called me. She said Morgan stormed out of there when Charlie told her about your request. Berta said she hadn't seen her that mad in years."

"Is that right?"

Morgan paused on the sidewalk, watching her breath frost around her. It was a beautiful day, clear and cold, the blue, blue sky seemingly endless, not even a hint of a cloud. Dare she blame the bright sunshine on her surprisingly good mood? A good mood despite the prospect of a ski trip tomorrow.

Reese Daniels could infuriate her one minute and take her breath away the next. And the story about her father? How tragic. Of course, Morgan could relate somewhat. Her own father was a fishing guide, and Morgan grew up helping crew the boat to wealthy clients, fishing both the Gulf of Mexico and the Atlantic. And she and her dad were as close as father and daughter could be. But that bond was shattered when she was twenty-one—twenty-one and gay. He never said it, but she suspected he blamed himself, as if hauling her all over the ocean in a smelly fishing boat had contributed to her being a lesbian. And it wasn't that they were estranged or anything. They spoke on the phone, they exchanged cards and letters, but there was always that gap between them, that chasm that they couldn't overcome. Her mother tried to be the bridge, but it was never enough. And being an only child, well, that too had shattered his dream of walking her down the aisle, of holding his first grandchild.

She took a deep breath, unconsciously reflecting on the past, watching the images flash by with lightning speed. She shrugged them away, taking another peek at the blue sky.

She felt different today. Gone was the restlessness, the monotony of winter, replaced with a contentment born of sharing herself with another person last night. Not a one-night stand, no. It felt completely different.

She smiled wryly. And so very, very different than the morning after with Moaning Mona.

CHAPTER TWENTY-ONE

Morgan pulled out a barstool, nodding at Tracy who was at the other end of the bar, taking a dinner order from Ernie Bates. It was quiet tonight, only a handful of the regulars around. Even the pool table was silent.

"Beer?"

"Please." She looked around. "Where is everyone?"

Tracy smiled. "The weather is supposed to be great tomorrow. Maybe they're like you. They have a skiing and fishing trip planned, so they're taking it easy."

Morgan rolled her eyes. "Very funny. And how did you hear about it?"

"Sloan heard it from Berta at lunch. Rumor has it you were very pissed and had a yelling match with Chief Daniels over at her office."

"You know how much I love skiing," she said, not really surprised that both Berta and Eloise had exaggerated the supposed *fight* between them.

"Speaking of," Tracy said, motioning to the door that had just opened. "Draw you a beer, Chief?" she called across the bar.

"Sure, Tracy." Reese sat down next to Morgan. "Good evening, Morgan. Are you in a better humor than the last time I saw you?"

Morgan stared at Reese's lips, watching as she fought to keep a smile away. "That depends. Have you come to cancel the trip?"

"Oh, no. I'm looking forward to it." She reached for her beer. "Thanks, Tracy."

"Dinner?"

"Something light. I have a busy day tomorrow."

"How about a chef's salad with grilled chicken?"

"Perfect."

"You're evil," Morgan said quietly when Tracy left them.

"Evil? And here I am thinking we need to work on that secret sign you mentioned."

"Is that right?"

"Yeah. Because if we had one, I'd use it about now."

Morgan shook her head. "And then expect me to be up at the crack of dawn to take you skiing? Think again, Chief."

"Just a thought. Because I really enjoyed being with you last night," she said, her voice low.

Morgan looked away, surprised at the quickening of her pulse. Yes, she'd enjoyed it too. Very much. But she hardly had the stamina to maintain *that* activity every night. Before she could reply, Tracy came back over.

"Your salad will be right out, Chief."

"Great."

Tracy wiped the water spots from their mugs, moving the glasses aside as she worked. It was something she did every night and Morgan wondered if she was even conscious of it.

"So, where are you taking the chief tomorrow, Morgan?"

Reese laughed. "You heard?"

"Oh, yeah. Nothing's a secret in this town."

Reese turned to her. "So, just where *are* you taking me?"

"Someplace with a high cliff. I may want to push you off."

Reese laughed, the sound filling the bar as the few other patrons there stopped and stared. Morgan couldn't help but smile, and knew they were doing a poor job of pretending to dislike each other.

"Why don't you take her up Alpine Meadow?" Tracy said. "It's an easy hike to the river."

"Easy? That's at least two miles."

"Two miles on skis is nothing, Morgan. Ed said he caught a big brown trout out of there a couple of weeks ago. And brook trout are easy to catch there. I think the chief would have fun."

Morgan narrowed her eyes. "This isn't about *the chief* having fun. This is about *me* having to *ski*."

Tracy smiled and backed up. "Maybe I better check on dinner."

"Maybe you better," Morgan muttered.

"So you're not going to be this cranky tomorrow, right?"

"Am I cranky?"

"A tad." Reese stood as Tracy came over with her salad. "Get to bed early, Morgan. Big day tomorrow."

Morgan scowled at her as she left, leaving Tracy laughing quietly.

"You know, it's a shame you two can't get along. I think you'd make a cute couple."

Morgan nearly spit her beer out. "For one thing, she's only here for a year, so there's no *couple* possibility. And two, she gets immense pleasure out of making my life miserable. There's just something wrong with that."

"You're like oil and water, I guess," Tracy said. "But still, you'd make a cute couple."

Morgan ignored her comment, instead sliding her empty mug down the bar. "I better get going. Like the chief said, big day tomorrow."

"Have fun. I hope you don't kill each other."

Morgan sat in her truck thinking no, they wouldn't kill each other. But she did wonder how long they could pull off this pretense that they really didn't like each other very much. Truth was, under any other circumstance, they would be on the verge of full-fledged dating. Their sense of humor mixed well, even though she would have sworn Reese Daniels *had* no sense of humor when they first met. They enjoyed each other's company, that was obvious. And after last night, it was quite evident they were completely compatible in bed.

So compatible, in fact, that Morgan wished she was there right now, having a repeat of last night.

She tapped the wheel with her fingers, indecisive. It was going to be a busy day tomorrow. She'd have to be up before dawn. But Reese had indicated she was game for a little get together tonight, secret sign or not.

So she drove away, not even looking down the side street that would take her to her house. She kept her eyes straight ahead as she drove out of town, feeling a bit shameless—and liking it.

CHAPTER TWENTY-TWO

Morgan sat in her truck for a long moment, staring at Reese's cabin. The light of the moon—nearly full—cast a bright reflection off the snow. She could see the smoke swirling out of the chimney, much as it had been last night. And that's where they'd ended up, on the rug by the fireplace, making love with such abandon, giving themselves freely without the restrictions of emotional ties. A physical, sexual relationship had its advantages.

And she wondered now if Reese was waiting for her. She'd no doubt seen her headlights, heard her truck. Was she by the door waiting, like she'd been last night?

Finally, the cold chased her out of the truck. She closed the door with a thud and walked through the snow to the front steps. It felt different than last night. Gone was the nervous feeling she'd carried with her, replaced by a desire that was a little bit disconcerting. It was a desire that—if left unchecked—could easily get out of control.

But that hardly mattered now. She raised her hand, knocking twice, waiting. And when Reese opened the door, their eyes met. There was no need for conversation. They both knew why she was here.

So she took Reese's hand and let herself be led into the dark bedroom. Reese turned on a small lamp, pushing the shadows away. Morgan stood there silently, her breath already coming fast as Reese came closer. Mutely, Reese undressed her, dropping the clothes beside the bed, then quickly shedding her own.

Morgan pulled the covers back on the bed and lay down, watching as Reese moved beside her, over her. Their eyes met and held, then Morgan's gaze slipped to Reese's lips that were so close, so inviting.

"I want to kiss you," Reese whispered.

Morgan shook her head. "No."

"No?" Reese lowered her head. "You don't want my tongue in your mouth?" She moved to Morgan's ear. "Like this?" she breathed, her tongue snaking in and out of her ear.

Morgan moaned and opened her legs, pulling Reese hard against her. God, *yes*, she wanted Reese's tongue in her mouth. She squeezed her eyes tight. But it was too intimate, too personal. Kissing, to her, was an emotional act, not a physical one. And it didn't belong in the arrangement they had. So she curbed her desire to feel Reese's lips on hers, to feel Reese's tongue slip into her mouth. Instead, she relished that tongue now as it bathed her ear, mimicking Reese's kisses. She moaned again as Reese moved her hips, thrusting gently against her, each stroke bringing them together, matching the rhythm her tongue had set. Morgan felt on fire and she opened her legs wider, welcoming Reese as she slammed against her clit, bringing her closer and closer to the edge as her tongue continued its assault. She heard herself grunting with each thrust of her hips but she didn't care. She was too close, too near climax to be concerned with the sounds Reese was pulling from her.

Harder and faster they rocked, Reese panting now in her ear as their hips slammed together, the slick wetness of their passion

115

mixing, the smell of sex and desire nearly overwhelming. So close, she could feel it, could taste it, could feel herself trembling, then tumbling over the edge, her hips jerking hard against Reese, trying to hold out, waiting for her. But she couldn't hold it another second and she exploded, her scream filling the bedroom, her last thrust against Reese bringing her over the edge as well as Reese groaned loudly in her ear, shifting so that they lay pressed together, their wetness soaking each other as their throbbing clits still touched.

"I thought I was going to pass out," she whispered.

"Me too," Reese said. "That was fantastic."

But before Morgan could recover, Reese slid her hand between their bodies, her fingers moving through her wetness, then slipping deep within her.

"Oh, God, no," Morgan murmured. "I can't, not this soon." But her hips moved, taking Reese inside her. She gripped Reese hard, holding on as she pounded into her, effortlessly bringing her again to orgasm, and Morgan bit down on Reese's shoulder as she climaxed for the second time in a matter of minutes.

Morgan collapsed on the bed, her arms limp at her side, her eyes shut. "You're trying to kill me."

"Hardly."

Morgan rolled her head to the side and opened her eyes, finding Reese there, her mouth only inches away. Her lips parted, waiting. Morgan pulled her gaze away, finding Reese's eyes instead. "No," she whispered.

"I just want to kiss you."

"No." Morgan forced herself up, smiling. "But I *do* want to kiss you," she whispered. Without ceremony or preamble, she cupped Reese's hips—bringing her to her mouth—and buried her face in her wetness, feasting on Reese as if she were starving. She took her hard, her tongue moving quickly across her clit, then sucking her fully into her mouth, suckling her as Reese squirmed beneath her.

She felt Reese's hands in her hair, her fingers twitching as Morgan took her to the edge again. Morgan held on tight as

Reese rose off the bed, her hips held high before collapsing in orgasm.

Morgan lifted her mouth away, letting herself be pulled up into Reese's arms. They lay together, holding each other as their breathing returned to normal. No words were spoken. Morgan felt her eyes sliding closed and knew she should get up, knew she should leave.

In a little while, she thought as she settled against Reese, her eyelids heavy.

CHAPTER TWENTY-THREE

Morgan wasn't sure she was happy to see Reese or not when she spotted the Sheriff's Department truck waiting for her at the trailhead the next morning. She'd already decided that if Reese wasn't there—it was five minutes after their agreed upon time already—she was leaving.

But no. A ski trip seemed inevitable as Reese smiled broadly at her.

"You're late."

Morgan arched an eyebrow. "And very tired. You must be too. Maybe we should call it off," she said.

"No, no. I feel great. Invigorated, in fact."

"How nice."

Reese came closer. "Don't you feel invigorated, Morgan?"

"I got home at three a.m. No, I don't feel invigorated. I need more than three hours sleep."

"I asked you to stay," Reese said. "Besides, you slept some

with me, didn't you?"

"I slept briefly. And how would I explain getting home at six?"

"It's winter. Who's out at that hour?"

"Randy Cummins works in Gunnison and is on the road by six, for one."

"Well, if someone saw you, you could always say you were up and on patrol early."

"Right. Like you said, it's winter." She pulled her pack from the back of her truck. "Even Googan takes it easy in the winter." She frowned as Reese stood there holding her skis. "Where's your gear?"

"What gear?"

"Your fishing gear."

Reese shook her head. "I don't have any fishing gear."

Morgan glared at her. "I'm out here at daybreak to take you fishing and you don't have any gear? Are you kidding me?"

"You're a little cranky this morning."

"You think?"

"Well, I thought, as the fishing guide, you would provide the gear," she said with an exaggerated smile.

"Fishing guide? You want a fishing guide, you hire Ed Wade and pay him a hundred bucks an hour to get up at daybreak," Morgan said loudly as she stomped around to the side of her truck for her skis. "Didn't bring gear," she mumbled. "Figures."

"What?"

"You heard me."

"You're going to try to throw me in the water, aren't you, Zula?"

"I wouldn't turn your back on me if I were you, *Clarice*."

Reese met her eyes. "Funny. Last night you wanted me to turn—"

Morgan held up her hand. "Don't go there."

Yes, last night she had wanted to do a lot of things with Reese Daniels. But that was last night. Today, with the prospect of a two-mile hike to the river, she wanted to throw Reese Daniels in the rushing stream.

But the trip across the meadow was easy, and after a few minutes, Morgan gave in as the beauty of the early morning penetrated her senses. The meadow was still pristine white from the snow, a sharp contrast to the dark green of the spruce and fir trees that lined the edges. In the spring, this meadow was a favorite spot as it came alive with the colors of wildflowers. And in fall, late in the evenings, this was where you came if you wanted to watch deer and elk forage before dark.

"I heard a rumor that Tracy fishes," Reese said, breaking the silence.

"No rumor. True. She's quite good and loves it. I think if she had a mind to, she could open up her own guide service." Morgan grinned. "Maybe you should get her to take you fishing from now on," she tossed over her shoulder, hearing Reese laugh.

"Eloise says she's turning thirty."

"That's true too."

"And never married?"

Morgan stopped, turning carefully with her skis. "I know where you're going with this, but she's straight. When Tracy and I became friends, her mother thought I was after her. She started bugging her to move to Gunnison, start college, be around people her own age."

"You're not much older. You said you're what? Thirty-six?"

"I'll be thirty-six in May. You?"

Reese nodded. "Thirty-seven."

"Anyway, Tracy's content here." Morgan shrugged. "Much like I am. The prospects of a romantic relationship are thin, but there are many other things in life. Tracy enjoys the outdoors. So working at Sloan's during the late shift gives her the opportunity to play all day."

"You mentioned her mother, so I guess she's from here?"

"Yep. Born and raised. Her two brothers work over at Thompson's Ranch, which is where most of the locals work. Those that don't cater to the tourists, that is. Or the handful who drive to Gunnison every day."

"Like Randy Cummins, who might spy you coming home from my place in the wee hours of the morning," Reese teased.

Morgan smiled. "See? You're learning."

They made the rest of the trip to the river in silence. Morgan was too absorbed in the beauty around her to offer conversation. She supposed Reese felt the same. As if their voices would disturb the splendor somehow.

But at the river's edge, they discarded their skis, the snow on the boulders nearly melted by the bright sunshine. The exertion from skiing had them both stripping off their lightweight jackets earlier. Now, Morgan pulled off her sweatshirt as well, leaving her in a long-sleeved flannel shirt, similar to the one Reese wore.

"Nice," Reese said as she watched her strip.

"Behave."

"I was talking about the river."

"Sure you were."

Reese smiled and turned her eyes to the rushing water. Morgan saw the smile fade from her face. She wondered if Reese could somehow feel her father's ghost. Before she could stop herself, she moved closer, slipping her arms across Reese's shoulders and pulling her into a tight hug. She felt Reese's warm breath on her neck and she closed her eyes, surprised at her body's reaction to such a platonic embrace. She backed away when her lips would have moved across Reese's skin.

"Thanks," Reese murmured. She tilted her head. "I vowed I would have nothing to do with boats or water. Or fishing ever again. Yet here I am."

"We don't have to fish."

"No. It's silly. Fishing didn't kill him."

"And *you* didn't kill him either," Morgan said firmly.

Reese squared her shoulders and took a deep breath. "I always loved to fish. I've missed it." She turned. "But you know, if it's all the same to you, I think I'll skip it this trip. I mean—"

"You don't have to explain. It's a beautiful morning, we had a pleasant, non-strenuous ski trip, and if you're up for it, we could ski down along the river for a bit."

"Why, Zula, are you actually suggesting more skiing?"

Morgan smiled. For some reason, Reese's use of her middle name wasn't annoying her today. But still, for appearance sake, "If you call me that one more time, I'm shoving you into the river."

"Idle threat, my love. Idle threat."

Morgan rushed forward and grabbed Reese's arms, playfully pushing her toward the water. But Reese spun them around and Morgan found herself holding on to Reese as she teetered near the edge.

"Don't you *dare*," Morgan shrieked as Reese leaned her backward over the water.

"Or what?" she teased.

"*Reese!*"

Reese smiled sweetly and pulled Morgan close, out of harm's way. "Do I get a kiss as my reward for saving you?"

"*Saving* me? I do believe you were the one *pushing* me." Morgan's eyes dropped to Reese's lips, which were dangerously close.

"You know, the more you tell me I can't kiss you, the more I want to."

"Yes, well, I have this rule, see. And kissing is *not* allowed," she said as she tried to pull out of Reese's arms.

"Tell me again why."

"You know why."

"What if I told you I wanted to break the rule?"

Morgan laughed. "Yes, I *know* you want to break the rule. But no."

"I'm a really good kisser."

"I don't doubt that. I have *some* idea of what your mouth can do, you know." Morgan felt her face flush as soon as the words were out of her mouth.

Reese's eyebrows shot up. "As do I. In fact, last night—"

Morgan covered Reese's mouth with her hand. "I will *not* talk about sex with you."

"You started it," Reese mumbled from behind Morgan's

hand.

She jerked her hand away when she felt Reese's tongue swipe across her palm. But as she turned, Reese's fingers wrapped around her arm, pulling her back. Dark eyes captured hers, holding her in place effortlessly. With her pulse pounding far too rapidly, Morgan looked beyond Reese, taking in the snowcapped mountain peaks, the dark green of the spruce trees. She even tried listening to the chatter of the gray jays and the insistent calling of the mountain chickadees. The fresh air, the crystal blue sky, the sounds of the forest…none of it could distract her from the woman who stood before her. A woman who wanted to kiss her. Her gaze settled on Reese's lips and she swallowed, her throat dry. It was at that very instant that she knew if she should allow a kiss between them, then all bets were off. She *wanted* her too much, she *enjoyed* her too much.

She raised her eyes to Reese's. "I'm not going to kiss you," she managed before turning away. She made a fist, hating how easily Reese could get her heart rate up. It was one thing, at night when they were alone, but not during the day, not when they were supposed to take a friendly hike on skis, not when there was nothing to their relationship but sex. She wasn't supposed to have to deal with these emotions. She wasn't supposed to *want* her this much. Or like it as much as she did.

"It's really very beautiful out here, isn't it?" Reese asked unexpectedly.

Morgan nodded, watching as Reese's gaze traveled along the river, then back to the meadow.

"I bet it's nice in the spring."

"The wildflowers are gorgeous, yes." Morgan walked back to where their skis were propped against a tree. "You want to ski down river?"

"If you're up to it, Zula," she said quietly behind her.

Morgan looked up, meeting her eyes, wondering how the name she hated most could sound almost like an endearment when Reese used it.

"I'm up for it, *Clarice*."

CHAPTER TWENTY-FOUR

Reese settled back in her chair, folding her hands behind her head and staring at her dark computer screen. Daybreak was still an hour away, but she couldn't sleep. After their hike, they had parted there in the meadow. And by nine that evening, with no word from Morgan, Reese had finally accepted the fact that she would be alone for the evening. But she slept fitfully, tossing around in the bed, feeling a restlessness she wasn't used to. Last night, she had refused to believe it had anything to do with Morgan's absence. But this morning?

She missed her. And not just the sex.

She got up and went into the main office for another cup of coffee. Well, missed her or not, it was what it was. Their arrangement was to get together *occasionally* for sex. There was no mention of companionship, of dinner, of watching a movie together. All normal things that two people who were dating would expect. Because they weren't dating.

She sipped her coffee, looking out onto the dark quiet street of downtown Lake City, knowing she was in for another uneventful day. Enough uneventful days made for an uneventful week. Christmas would come and go in eight days time, then the new year. And then they'd be stuck in the middle of winter, *hunkering down*, as Eloise said, to wait it out. Spring came slowly up here. Or so she was told. And by April, if she'd survived, the spring thaw would begin. And spring brought warmer weather, bright flowers, green grass. And spring brought summer. And summer brought the tourists and an end to uneventful days.

She wondered if summer would also bring an end to her and Morgan's arrangement.

I hope not.

Morgan hung her jacket on the coat rack in the corner after a curt nod at Berta who already had her knitting stuff out. It was a sign of the slow days of winter when Berta spent most of her time working on her latest afghan. She glanced into Charlie's office, seeing the newspaper spread out.

"Morning," she called as she pulled out her chair.

"How was skiing?"

Morgan glanced at Berta and made a face at her. "Skiing was skiing. At least it wasn't cold."

"Fishing?"

"No."

"I thought that was the point."

"She didn't have gear and thought I would supply it. As if I'm a freakin' guide," she added, hoping her tone sounded as annoyed as she intended it to be.

"If she doesn't want Ed Wade, she should ask Tracy," Berta said.

"Yes, I told her the next time she got a wild hair about fishing, not to call me." Morgan rummaged in her backpack, finding the bottle of ibuprofen she kept in there at all times. She was three days early, but she'd started her period this morning. And along with that came cramps. And bloating. And maybe she was just a tiny bit irritable. That irritability was what prevented her from going to Reese's last night. That and the fact that she thought the whole situation was becoming a little, well, uncomfortable. After only a few days together, she was already losing her grasp on the *no strings* arrangement. Because it felt too much like they were dating, too much like it was normal, and far too *right* to be together. The sex was effortless…natural. So she'd stayed away last night, trying to put a little distance between them.

CHAPTER TWENTY-FIVE

Reese heard the bell jingle and listened for a familiar voice. Another night had come and gone and still no word from Morgan. She thought perhaps she might just pop over for a visit, but it was a man's voice she heard.

"Sure, she's in. Go on back."

Reese frowned. It was unlike Eloise to just send anyone back without letting her know. She stood as a large man filled her doorway.

"Chief Daniels," he greeted her, his voice loud. He stuck his hand out. "I'm Ron Brightmen, nice to finally meet you."

She took his hand and nodded. "Right. I'm living in your cabin. Thanks."

He sat in the visitor's chair without asking, motioning for Reese to have a seat. Reese remained standing.

"What can I do for you, Mr. Brightmen?"

"Oh, I just wanted to visit with you a bit. As one of the

commissioners, consider it a welcoming party," he said with a laugh.

"Well, I've been here two months so you're a little late."

"Sorry about that. Fall's my busiest time of year. I have an outfitting service, so we have a lot of out-of-state hunters who come up here. I'm sure you've heard of my place, the B and B Resort up above the lake there."

She shook her head as she settled back into her chair. "No, I haven't heard of it."

"Oh, well, we don't really do business with the locals." He laughed. "I suppose most of them are pissed off about it anyway. I have my own little store up there, a restaurant, the hunting cabins. No need for my clients to even come down into town for supplies."

"You're a county commissioner yet you get pleasure from taking business away from the locals? I'm surprised you get reelected."

"I get reelected because I have more money than anyone in the county other than Stuart Thompson."

"So he's a commissioner too?"

"Yep. Me and Stuart and Michael Turner."

"And what does Mr. Turner do?"

"He owns the Mountaintop RV Resort, going up Cinnamon Pass."

"Yes, I've been by there. Nice place."

"Yeah, he's full up every summer." He leaned forward. "I really came by to thank you," he said.

"Thank me for what?"

"Taking the job, for one thing. We were hard-pressed when Ned decided to leave in the middle of his term. We didn't think we'd find anyone to take his place. And the thought of Googan being interim sheriff for two years wasn't appealing to anyone." He held out his hand again. "If there's anything you need, anything we can do for you, you just let me know."

She shook his hand, then glanced at the card he'd casually tossed on her desk. "Thanks, Mr. Brightmen, but as you know,

I'm only here for the one year. If his term is not up for two, then I guess you'll have Googan to deal with interim after all."

"We're hoping you change your mind about that. You may not be a local and no one knows you, but come election time, they'd all vote for you over Googan." He laughed. "Because they *do* know Googan."

He left as quickly as he'd come in, bidding a quick *good day* to Eloise before the jingle of the bell signaled his leaving. She picked up his card, turning it over in her hand, seeing his scribbled cell phone number on the back. She let out a deep breath, then tossed the card into her drawer. She couldn't imagine the county producing a whole lot of revenue, and she suspected the allocation they got from the state was small seeing as how the population of the county was less than a thousand souls. Most likely, Brightmen and Thompson footed the bill, which was why they got reelected. The locals may resent them, but they also knew they needed them. That was how politics worked in small towns.

But, not her concern, she reminded herself. Ten more months and she was free to leave. But in the meantime…

She picked up the phone and dialed the Forest Service office, listening patiently as Berta greeted her.

"It's Chief Daniels. Is Morgan in?" she asked politely.

"Chief Daniels for you," Berta called across the room.

Morgan looked blankly at the phone, then glanced back at Berta who was staring at her. She couldn't just ignore it, even if she wanted to. So she summoned her most professional tone as she answered.

"Morgan here, may I help you?"

"Hi, Zula."

Morgan gritted her teeth. "Chief Daniels."

"I haven't seen you around lately. I'm wondering if I've done something to upset you."

Morgan turned her back to Berta, only to find herself staring at Charlie who watched from his office. Good grief. Could she not have one moment of privacy? "I'm fine," she said.

"Can't talk?"

"Right."

"Shame. I wanted to tell you how much I've missed you and that I can't wait to see you naked again and that I want you to come over tonight so I can make love to you."

"Is that right?"

"Absolutely. But since you can't talk, how would I know if you want to make love to me?"

Morgan closed her eyes, hating the fact that her heart was racing. Damn the woman. She looked up at Berta who was still watching her. "It's nearly lunch. Do you want to meet at Sloan's and we can discuss it?"

"I'm on my way."

Morgan smiled as she hung up. Yes, she'd stayed away from Reese Daniels on purpose. Getting her period was as good an excuse as any. But both nights as she'd paced restlessly in her cabin she'd had to force herself to stay home. And apparently Reese had missed her. She stood, scooting her chair back and slinging her backpack over her shoulder.

"I'm going to Sloan's," she said.

Berta just nodded and Morgan knew as soon as she was out the door, Berta would be on the phone. First with Eloise, then with Tina, filling her in. She didn't know why they were trying to keep their affair a secret. She knew speculation was already running rampant among the locals.

And there Reese was, waiting for her, impatiently tapping the table as she lounged in a corner booth, two glasses of tea in front of her.

"You're evil," Morgan said as she slid in across from her.

Reese laughed. "Sorry. Couldn't help it. And I ordered you a grilled cheese. Jeff said it was your usual."

"Thanks." Morgan stared at her, trying to recall exactly why it was she'd stayed away. Because Reese's eyes were friendly, open, her lips relaxed in a smile. And yeah, she'd missed her too. "I started my period," Morgan blurted out.

Reese's eyebrows rose.

"Sorry." Morgan leaned her elbows on the table. "That's why I didn't come over," she said. It was somewhat the truth.

"You could have still come over. We don't always have to have sex, Morgan," she said quietly. "We can watch a movie or…or share a meal together. You don't have to stay away because of that."

Morgan shook her head. "That's too much like dating," she said. "And I think that was one of your stipulations. You didn't want to date anyone. You were just looking for sex."

Reese leaned back against the seat. "I did say that, didn't I?" She shrugged. "Seeing as how I'm leaving after a year, dating wouldn't really be fair anyway."

"Right."

"That still doesn't mean we can't see each other. You know, as friends. Unless you're only interested in my company if sex is involved."

"No. I happen to enjoy your company. Truth is, well, I get a little cranky when I start my period. I thought it best to spare you," Morgan said with a quiet laugh. It was true. She did enjoy Reese's company, sex or not. She liked the fact that they could tease each other in a friendly manner, even with the underlying sexual tension that seemed to follow them. Even now, sitting with her in a very public place, when their eyes met, there was that familiarity that only existed between lovers.

"Cranky or not, why don't you come over tonight? I'd offer you dinner, but we've already discussed my limitations there."

"You know, there *is* a grocery store in town."

"Yes. I pass by it every day. In fact, I've stopped in a couple of times for necessities like chips and peanut butter."

"Okay, I'll confess. My lack of cooking has nothing to do with not knowing how and everything to do with hating it."

"So you do cook?"

"Yes, I can. I think I hate it because my mother used to insist on giving me cooking lessons when I was a kid. Instead of being outside playing, I was stuck in the kitchen, cutting up vegetables, browning hamburger meat and learning how to make spaghetti sauce from scratch."

"Homemade spaghetti sauce?"

"Let's start with something simple. Like a casserole or something, hmm?"

"You tell me what to buy and I'll go by the grocery store," Reese said. "What about wine? The liquor store down the street always has a closed sign. Are they out of business?"

Morgan shook her head. "No. But in the winter, they only open on Saturday. Come May, they'll be back to regular hours. But I have a couple of bottles. I'll bring one."

"Now see, isn't this nice? Planning a dinner with no mention of sex."

"So you think I'm going to cook for free?"

Reese leaned closer. "If you're game, we can work around your *crankiness*." Reese met her eyes. "I would hate to miss an opportunity to be with you."

Morgan felt the fluttering of her pulse and she reached for her tea. She always got a visual whenever Reese mentioned them being together. A visual that included them both naked and wet. *Good grief*. She wondered what her reaction would be if they really *were* dating. Reese had a smooth, sensual voice that sent shivers down her spine. Thankfully, she was saved from responding when Jeff brought over their lunch.

"Hi, Morgan. Hope the grilled cheese is okay," he said as he put the plate in front of her, a generous portion of fries piled beside the sandwich.

"Perfect, Jeff. Thanks." She raised her eyebrows as a salad with grilled chicken was placed in front of Reese. "Tired of burgers?"

"I was having vegetable withdrawal, I think. Thanks, Jeff."

"Sure thing. Let me know if you need anything else."

"Why don't he and Tracy hook up?" Reese asked when he left them. "They're about the same age, aren't they?"

Morgan nodded. "They're also cousins. They both refer to him as Uncle Sloan."

"So both born and raised here and never left?"

"No, Jeff went to college. Went to Ft. Lewis in Durango but didn't finish. When he came back, Sloan gave him a job so he wouldn't have to work at Thompson's Ranch," she said as she took a bite of her sandwich. "This is so good. And so fattening."

"I almost ordered one myself," Reese said. "Speaking of Thompson's Ranch, Ron Brightmen came to see me this morning."

"Oh yeah? I didn't know they were back."

"Back from where?"

"They fly to the Bahamas each year after hunting season. That's their busiest time at the B and B. Although they're packed during the summer too."

"I got the impression he and Thompson run things in the county."

"For sure. But they have money, they have connections. We have the smallest population of any county in the state, by far, yet we don't lack for state funds when it comes to road repairs and the like. Even as isolated as we feel in the winter, they've managed to make sure snowplows don't forget about us after a storm. Making financial contributions to state lawmakers has its advantages."

"Yet he's got his own mini-town up at his resort?"

Morgan laughed. "He likes to think he does. He hired some big-time chef from Denver to head up his restaurant, but it's all Italian fare. His hunters flock down here to Sloan's on steak night." She chewed on a fry. "Why did he come see you?"

"Just to introduce himself and to thank me for taking the job."

"He doesn't know about the mayor's wife, does he?" she teased.

"I'm guessing not."

"So he was thanking his lucky stars that Googan wasn't sheriff?"

Reese nodded. "Pretty much, yeah. And I know Googan is a bit out of his league, but he's surely not that much of a Barney

Fife, is he?"

Morgan's eyes widened. "You don't let him have bullets for his gun, do you?"

"I assume he does. He's a deputy, isn't he?"

"I'm surprised Eloise didn't fill you in. Ned let him carry a gun, but he couldn't keep it loaded. He kept a clip in his car under the seat for emergencies," she said.

"What happened to cause that?"

Morgan laughed. "It's funny now, but it could have been very tragic." She shoved her plate aside after dipping a fry in ketchup. "One night he was out on patrol and saw a light on at Lou's Grocery. Well, it had been a busy summer day with lots of tourists in town, so he had it in his mind that someone was breaking in. No, it was just Lou sneaking over for some ice cream. But Googan burst in right about the time Lou turned out the light. He fired six rounds into the store."

"Oh, my God."

"Shot the glass out of the cooler door, shot the cash register, fired twice into the freezer. Then he got turned around and shot out the front store window, the bullet going into his truck, shattering the glass there. The final shot went into the ceiling."

Reese laughed. "But I'm assuming Lou wasn't hurt?"

"Not hurt but plenty pissed. The county footed the bill on the repairs obviously, but the only way Googan kept his job was to agree to no bullets. That was six years ago."

"So you're saying I need to inspect his weapon to see if he's got it loaded?"

"I would."

"And he's going to be your next sheriff, huh?"

Morgan rolled her eyes. "I doubt they'll let it come to that. *They* meaning Brightmen and Thompson. They'll talk somebody into running against Googan."

"And does Googan know how everyone feels?"

"He probably doesn't have a clue." Morgan leaned her elbows on the table and rested her chin on her hands. "How does beef stroganoff sound?"

"For dinner?"

"Yes."

"You can make that?"

"It's not difficult. I have a nice bottle of merlot that'll go good with it."

"And you're going to send me shopping?"

"I'll handle that too. I have a hard time picturing you shopping for food."

Reese reached across the table and stole a fry from her plate, her eyes twinkling as she popped it in her mouth.

CHAPTER TWENTY-SIX

"Corkscrew?"

Reese frowned. "Can't say that I've seen one here." She pulled out a drawer in the kitchen and rummaged through it, then stopped. "I've got a Swiss Army knife." She grinned. "It's always good for something, isn't it?"

Morgan laughed, watching her hurry into her bedroom and return with the familiar red knife. "Perfect."

"Do you think anyone actually uses this thing as a knife?"

Morgan pulled out the corkscrew and carefully fitted it, twisting it tightly into the cork. She handed it to Reese. "You can do the honors," she said as she went back to the stove to drain the egg noodles.

"That smells great, by the way."

Morgan smiled as she heard the distinctive pop of the cork being released. "Beef stroganoff is easy to make. It just sounds hard. Besides, this is the poor man's version." Morgan nodded as Reese pointed to the wineglass. "Instead of ground beef, you should use sirloin or tenderloin cut thin. And fresh mushrooms instead of canned."

"But Lou was out?"

"Yeah. Fresh vegetables are iffy during the winter. Depends on the weather whenever the truck is scheduled to come down from Gunnison. Plus Lou doesn't like to order as much when there's only the locals shopping. There's just not that many of us."

"And I guess some make the trip to Gunnison to shop?"

"Oh, yeah. Some can't live without their Wal-Mart fix." She piled two plates high with noodles, then covered them with the beef stroganoff mixture and added a spoonful of green beans on the side. "Ready?"

"Starving."

Morgan was touched by the table Reese had set. With the lights turned down, two candles lit the table, and she touched glasses with Reese in a silent salute. "Cozy," she said.

"I was shooting for romantic," Reese said.

"Okay, it is romantic. I just didn't want to say that if you were only shooting for cozy," she teased.

Reese moaned as she took her first bite of dinner and Morgan was secretly pleased.

"Oh, my God," Reese mumbled with a mouthful. "This is so good."

"Thank you. Every cook likes to hear that." She sipped her wine. "The moans help too."

Reese smiled as she took another bite. "I'm in heaven. I've lived on Sloan's food since I got here. My taste buds are doing the happy dance."

"I eat a lot of soup in the winter," Morgan said. "Canned though. And I know I should cook more, but it's just such a chore to do it for one person."

"Well, now there's two of us. Let that be motivation for you," Reese said as she pointed to her plate. "Because this is delicious."

"I guess I could make an effort to cook occasionally. But don't expect it every night."

"It?" Reese grinned. "What *it* are we talking about?"

Morgan laughed. "Yeah, don't expect *it* every night either."

They ate in silence for a moment, then as Reese refilled their wineglasses, she said, "Tell me about Jackson."

Morgan looked up, surprised. She had only mentioned Jackson once. She hadn't thought Reese remembered.

"Jackson was, well, he was my friend," she said, embarrassed by the welling of tears. She looked away. "Sorry. But I miss him."

"It's okay. Tell me about him."

Morgan thought back on the day she got him and smiled. Her first dog. "It was a spur-of-the-moment thing and one of the best decisions I ever made," she said. "I got transferred out to the desert in Arizona. BLM land, very remote. I was told the winters would be busy, as RVers congregated there to wait out the cold. But the summers were long, hot and lonely. So, the day before I left, I found an ad for Labrador puppies. I'd never had a dog before, but I thought I needed some sort of companion if I was going to be stuck out in the middle of nowhere." She laughed. "And you think Lake City is remote."

"I've heard of Quartsite in Arizona, where they have RV orgies," Reese said. "Were you near there?"

"About eighty miles away, but the same concept." Morgan put her fork down and picked up her wineglass instead. "He was seven weeks old when I got him. And we arrived at our new post just as the wintering RVs were leaving. And the summer was long and hot. But not really lonely as Jackson and I got to know one another. And a big plus were the springs. Jackson loved the water, and it was the only place to cool off. We pretty much had the summer to ourselves. There was only the occasional camper. By October, the RVs started coming back. It was quite the reverse from what we have here. October to April down there was far busier than our summers are here. But the rest of the year, it was just brutal. I lasted four full seasons, then transferred to Colorado.

I was supposed to be in the Gunnison district at Blue Mesa but got sent to Lake City at the last moment." She shrugged. "After the initial shock, it really was the best thing. The little house I have, it's right at the edge of the forest. Jackson loved the freedom he had here. If we'd been in Gunnison, he'd have been in a yard in town."

"So he had a good life."

"Yeah, he did. And he made mine all the better."

"But you're not ready for another one?"

She shook her head. "I'm not sure I'll ever be ready. We were so close. I feel like I lost a part of my family, and I'm not sure I can replace that."

Reese took their plates to the sink and rinsed them. "I've never had a pet," she said. "Even as kids, we never had a pet around the house." She pointed at the stove. "You're going to let me keep this for leftovers, right?"

"It's all yours." Morgan got up and brought their wineglasses to the sink. "All done with the wine?"

"I think so. Unless you want some more."

"No, I'm good." She covered her mouth as a yawn escaped. "Sorry."

"Go relax while I clean up," Reese said.

"I should really get going. If I sit down, I might fall asleep."

"You can stay here tonight, you know."

But Morgan shook her head. "I'm not up for it tonight, Reese. Besides, you know, I'm still—"

"I know, Morgan. And you must think I'm a sex monster or something. I just meant you could stay here. *Sleep* here," she said. "I've enjoyed your company. And I've missed you."

Morgan stared at her, somewhat surprised by Reese's admission that she'd missed her. Not missed having sex, but missed her being around. It occurred to her then that an arrangement of a physical relationship of sex without ties would work much better if the two parties involved didn't really like each other. But in their case, their friendship was growing stronger, thus making the sexual part of their relationship less physical and more emotional.

And that thought scared the hell out of her.

Morgan turned, pulling out of Reese's arms and squinted at the clock. Five fifteen. She closed her eyes again, knowing she should leave, but it was too warm under the covers and she was far too comfortable right where she was.

"What time is it?" Reese whispered in her ear.

Morgan sighed and snuggled closer to her warmth. "After five," she murmured. She felt Reese's lips caress her skin.

"Living dangerously, aren't you?"

Morgan rolled toward Reese, pressing their bodies together. "It's nice and warm here. I don't want to get up." She moaned as Reese's hands slid across her body, cupping her buttocks and squeezing. "Don't start," she whispered.

"It was your idea to sleep naked."

"I always sleep naked," she said, then moaned again as Reese's lips nipped at her throat. "We can't do this." She stopped Reese's hand before she could capture her breast. "I should go."

"I want to kiss you."

"Oh, no, you don't." Morgan groaned and turned away. It was getting too hard. She wanted to kiss her. She wanted to touch her. She wanted to make love to her this morning. Instead, she pulled out of her arms. "I should go," she said again. She heard Reese sigh and felt her slip away from her.

"I know."

Morgan tossed the covers off and hurried into her sweatshirt, the morning chill making her shiver.

"You want me to get a fire going?"

"No, no. I'm fine. Go back to sleep." She turned, pulling the covers around Reese again.

"Thank you for staying last night," Reese said sleepily. "It was nice."

Morgan nodded. "Yes. I like sleeping with you too." But Reese's even breathing told her she was fast asleep again. She watched her for a moment longer, her eyes drawn to her lips. Without thinking, she bent closer and gave her the barest of kisses. But it was enough for her to want more. She made herself move away from Reese and she pulled her eyes from her lips, needing all her willpower to walk out of the room when what she really wanted was to crawl back in bed with her.

She shut the bedroom door quietly, then leaned back against it and closed her eyes. Yes, she had stayed the night. Yes, they had slept naked. And no, they hadn't had sex. They'd cuddled together like two people in the midst of a lovely courtship... touching, but never crossing the boundary as they drifted off to sleep. And a wonderful sleep it was as they held each other during the night.

She pushed away from the door, telling herself she was still in control of the situation. It was only natural to have some emotional attachment to the person you're having sex with. *Right?*

Right.

CHAPTER TWENTY-SEVEN

"Good morning, Eloise," Reese said as she walked into her office.

"Chief," Eloise murmured, not looking up from the morning paper.

Reese paused. "Where's Googan?"

Eloise looked up then. "Why?"

Reese arched an eyebrow. "Because I'm the chief, he's the deputy and you're the *secretary*, and I want to know where he is." She pointed at the radio. "You want to rouse him up for me?"

"He's got a cell phone," she mumbled as she picked up the radio. "Googan, you copy? The chief's looking for you." When there was no answer, Eloise said, "You know, it's barely eight. Maybe he's—"

"It's nearly eight thirty."

"He may have worked the night shift."

"What night shift?" She pointed at the phone. "Call his

cell."

"Gee, wish I'd thought of that."

Reese hid a smile as Eloise dialed. She was in a feisty mood this morning, Reese noted.

"Googan? Where are you?" Eloise looked at Reese. "I see. Well, the chief is wanting to talk to you." Eloise's eyes widened. "Yes," she said slowly, sliding her gaze to Reese.

Reese rolled her eyes and took the phone from Eloise. "Googan? Where the hell are you?"

"Chief Daniels...I...well, I must have overslept," he said, his voice still hoarse. "I was out late last night. On patrol, you know."

"On patrol, huh? I haven't seen you in three days. Now get your ass in here." She slammed the phone down. "On patrol my ass," she muttered under her breath as she went into her office. "What's he patrolling? Watching the ice form on the lake?"

"You want coffee?"

"I'll get it, Eloise. Don't let me keep you from your daily paper."

"Well, you're in a mood," Eloise said just loud enough for her to hear.

Was she in a mood? Perhaps. Her fond memory of snuggling with Morgan early that morning had faded when she woke up alone. Alone and cold, and to an empty house. She couldn't believe how quickly Morgan's presence—or lack of—had affected her life. She was used to being alone. And she certainly wasn't used to having only one sexual partner. Not even when she and Julie had been somewhat a couple all those years ago. Because they weren't *really* a couple. Julie worked in vice. Reese in narcotics. Their relationship was more of a stress relief than anything else. And after three years, they just started drifting apart, their time together less and less until it stopped altogether. That was the only time in her life she even came close to having a relationship with someone.

Not that she considered what she and Morgan had as a relationship. *Affair* would more properly describe it. An affair

Morgan wanted to keep a secret. Which in some ways belittled it. But when you make an agreement for a physical, sexual arrangement without all the hassle of emotional ties, there wasn't a whole lot of basis to it anyway. It was just sex. Two people performing an act.

That's how it was intended, anyway. But last night, as they slept together, holding each other, there was no sex, there was no act. And if she were honest, there was nothing physical or sexual about it. Emotional? Yes. Because she felt a connection with Morgan that went deeper than just the sexual involvement they'd agreed to. She suspected the same was true for Morgan.

She spun around in her chair and stared out the window, wondering if maybe they needed to curb things. Slow down a bit. Maybe do like Morgan had suggested in the beginning. Just get together once a week.

She sighed. She wanted more than once a week. The sexual attraction between them was too strong. Unfortunately, the emotional attraction was rearing its head as well. An attraction that made Reese crave not once a week with Morgan, but every day.

It was a dangerous craving, she knew.

But she had no more time to contemplate their affair as she heard the bell jingle and then Googan's distinct voice as he greeted Eloise.

"Come on back, Googan," Reese called. He shuffled down the short hallway, pausing at her door. "Sit down. Close the door."

He shifted nervously as he crossed the threshold. "What's up, Chief?"

She motioned him in. "Just come in, Googan. Close the door."

"If you're pissed about me oversleeping—"

"It has nothing to do with that." She pointed at the chair. "Now sit down." He finally settled into one of the visitor's chairs. She leaned back in her chair and crossed her arms, watching him. "I have a concern, Googan."

"What's that?"

"There was an incident at Lou's Grocery several years ago. You want to tell me about that?"

His face turned red and he looked away. "I'm sure you've heard."

"I haven't heard your version."

"I don't really have a version. It happened so fast, and I guess I just panicked. I was in the wrong," he said quietly.

"I see. And what was the result of that incident?"

"What do you mean?"

"You know what I mean, Googan." She sat up. "Let me see your weapon."

"Why?"

She held out her hand, waiting. He finally moved, the leather of his belt creaking as he shifted, unsnapping the strap that held his gun in place. He pulled it out then handed it to her butt first. It was a standard issue police duty weapon, Smith and Wesson. She released the magazine, the clip sliding easily into her hand. The clip was full. It had also been topped off with one in the chamber.

"What the hell, Googan?"

"I'm a goddamn police officer," he said loudly. "I should be able to—"

"Shut up," she said as she laid the gun and magazine clip on her desk. "You're a sheriff's deputy with very little training. That's the bottom line. You want to be a goddamn police officer, but you're not." She held up her hand when he would have spoken. "However, the fact that my predecessor let you carry a weapon without ammunition is just crazy." She stood and went to the window, looking out. "What do you think we should do, Googan?"

"I don't know."

She glanced at him. "Can't have my deputy unarmed now, can I?" She shrugged. "You plan on getting this job when I'm gone?"

"Yes."

"Then you're going to need some training."

"But I've been to—"

"Apparently not enough," she said. "You can't just *want* to be a police officer, Googan. There's more to the job than just sitting in this chair and saying you're the Sheriff of Hinsdale County." She smiled. "The fact that we carry weapons at all is laughable considering we haven't had a police incident in the current century."

"But—"

"I know, I know. This isn't Mayberry." She sighed. "Take your weapon, Googan. Keep the clip. But for God's sake, don't top it off by keeping one in the chamber. You could shoot yourself in the goddamn leg if you hit a bump in the road."

"You mean I can keep the bullets?"

"Like you said, you're a police officer. However, in this case, I think it would have been wise for you to tell me about your previous restrictions. Don't you?"

"I didn't want you to think I was incapable of doing the job."

"I don't base qualifications on what others say, good or bad. But I'll find some training sessions for you. Winter's a good time, seeing as how slow it is." She sat down again. "Now, let's talk about why you were in bed at eight thirty in the morning. And spare me the bullshit about being on patrol last night. We don't have a patrol, Googan. It's winter. There's nothing to patrol."

"I was playing poker with some of the guys. It got late."

She laughed. "Now that's more like it. I know there's nothing going on now, Googan. No tourists around to hassle. No speeders coming over the pass. But it's our job just to have a presence in town. What I'm saying is, don't let three days go by without showing your face around here again."

"But I've been around. I just didn't see the point of coming in here and sitting."

"Well, humor me by coming in, will you?" She motioned to the door. "Now, how about some daytime patrol, huh?"

"Sure, Chief." Googan paused at the door as he snapped his weapon back into the holster. "I...I appreciate it, Chief Daniels."

He patted his gun. "I won't do anything stupid."

"No. I don't believe you will." She motioned out the window. "It's starting to snow. Be careful out there."

He nodded then headed out, his head held a little higher than when he'd come in. Sure, she had reservations. Based on what everyone said, Googan was just a big kid wanting to play cop. But she could see in his eyes he had the drive. He'd just never been nurtured. Most likely the only training Ned Carter insisted on was the basics. He learned how to fire his weapon and was taught what all the controls in his police vehicle were. That's it. If he planned to man the town after she left, he'd need some training. It was the least she could do for Lake City.

CHAPTER TWENTY-EIGHT

Morgan slammed the door to the office and shook the snow off her shoulders. "Man, it's really coming down," she said.

"Temperatures are funky," Charlie said. "Going to be more ice than snow."

"It's windy as hell."

"Where you been?"

Morgan shrugged off her coat and hung it on the coatrack in the corner. "I drove up the pass. It's sticking pretty good up there. I think Chief Daniels should close the road."

"Not that there's anyone going to be traveling," Charlie said. "Berta, why don't you head on home? No sense in hanging around here."

"Don't have to tell me twice," she said as she gathered up her knitting.

"And call in the morning. If it's bad, let's call a snow day," he said.

Morgan raised her eyebrows. "Does that go for all of us?"

"Oh, hell, Morgan, it's almost Christmas. There's nothing going on. As long as one of us is here, I think we're covered."

She pulled out her chair and sat down, jiggling her mouse to clear her screen saver. "I thought this was just a dusting," she said as she pulled up a weather site. "I don't know why we even bother with forecasts."

"I usually avoid them myself," Charlie said. "You know I just rely on you guys to keep me informed. But less than a week until Christmas, a good snowstorm is always welcome."

"You know Tina is leaving in a couple of days, don't you?"

"Leaving where?"

"Her mother-in-law decided on a Florida Christmas this year. They're leaving on the twenty-second."

"Flying out of where?"

"They're taking a jumper from Gunnison down to Albuquerque." She clicked on the bookmark for Gunnison's weather. "Damn, we might get a couple of feet."

"Oh, well. Good for the trails," he said as he went back into his office. "With Tina gone, what are you going to do at Christmas?"

Morgan shrugged. It was common knowledge that she spent every holiday with Tina and her family. In fact, Charlie usually joined them as well. But this year? There was Reese. Morgan doubted she'd even given Christmas a thought. "What are you going to do, Charlie?"

"I'm thinking I'm going to go south for a week or so. Maybe get in some fishing."

"South where?"

'You know my buddy Allen, he retired and moved out near Tucson."

"He's the one who lost his wife last year, right?"

"Yeah. I thought I might go down for a visit. I hate to leave you here alone though, what with Tina gone."

"Oh, Charlie, I'll be fine. You know me and holidays."

"You sure?"

"Absolutely. Make your plans. I've got it covered."

And she did. Even if Reese had other plans—which she doubted—she'd still be fine. She'd spent the holidays alone before. So if not with Reese, she'd at least take the opportunity to rent a snowmobile from the Pattersons and hit the trails.

She glanced into Charlie's office, hearing him on the phone with Allen. It was nice to see the relaxed smile on his face. In the seven years she'd been here, he'd never taken a vacation, only stealing a few days here and there to do some fishing. It would do him good to get away for a week.

She sighed, looking around her very neat desk, trying to think of something to do to occupy her afternoon. This time of year, the hours just crept by, and you could only surf the Internet so long without going stir-crazy. She jiggled the mouse again, wondering if she'd end up like Berta and eventually take up knitting.

No.

So she browsed Web sites, checked the weather, read the Denver paper online and answered an e-mail from her mother. *No, she wouldn't be able to make Christmas this year.* And as a last resort, she played solitaire.

She was just about to shut down and head out when Charlie hurried out of his office.

"Do you have your scanner on?"

"No. Why?"

"Some kind of accident. Dead Man's Ridge."

"Oh, no. Surely someone didn't go over?" She grabbed her backpack. "Was it a local? What did you hear?" She frowned as he reached out a hand to her. "Charlie?"

"It was a sheriff's vehicle."

"Oh, my God." She panicked. "Reese?" She took a deep breath. "Or Googan?"

"I don't know, Morgan. I tried calling, but Eloise didn't answer."

"I'm going out there," she said quickly as she brushed by him. "Googan's driven that road a thousand times. He knows the curves. Reese wouldn't."

"You don't need to go out there, Morgan. Obviously, the roads are bad. You'll just get in the way."

"No. I won't get in the way."

She let the door slam behind her and nearly slipped on the sidewalk as she hit a patch of ice. Her hands were shaking as she started her truck and flipped on the headlights. Darkness came early in the winter, especially on a snowy day like today. She drove as fast as she dared, slowing down at each curve. Yes, she'd driven Dead Man's Ridge a thousand times too. There was no guardrail on top. Hell, there wasn't room to put a guardrail. It was simply a sheer drop into the canyon.

She felt guilty for hoping it was Googan and not Reese, but she couldn't help it. The thought of Reese tumbling off the side, her truck free falling into the canyon made her sick to her stomach. When she hit the last switchback going up the mountain, she could see the flashing emergency lights at the top of the ridge and her heart skipped a beat.

"Oh, please, Reese," she whispered. She didn't pause to consider the extent of her anxiety as she drove slowly up the hill, her hands gripped tight on the wheel.

CHAPTER TWENTY-NINE

Reese laid flat on her stomach, inching to the edge of the road and peering over the side. The darkness was moving in quickly, but she was able to make out the hulk of Googan's truck. It appeared to be upright, not flipped on its side. Or worse, upside down.

"Anything?"

She backed up and got to her knees, taking Ed Wade's hand and letting herself be pulled to her feet. "I can barely see the truck, much less movement. What's the word from Thompson's ranch?"

"They've got a truck with a winch. A hundred feet. That ought to get you down far enough to hit the ledge. Then another thirty feet or more to climb down." He raised his eyebrows. "With the snow and ice, it could be very dangerous for you too, Chief."

"No other choice. It'll be another half hour or more before fire and rescue gets here from Gunnison." She looked up as headlights approached from down the mountain, from town.

"Let me stop this truck," she said as she hurried off. "Can you turn your car around and face the edge? Any extra light'll help," she called.

She walked in the middle of the road, waving her hands at the approaching truck. Her brows drew together when she saw that it was Morgan. She hurried over and opened the door, seeing Morgan's frightened eyes.

"Morgan, the road is terrible. You shouldn't be out in this."

"I'm...I'm sorry. I just—"

Reese took her arm and pulled her out of her truck. "What's wrong?"

"Charlie heard on the scanner, but we didn't know—"

Reese finally understood and she pulled Morgan into a tight hug, not caring that Ed Wade was most likely watching them.

"And you thought it was me," she said quietly into Morgan's ear. She felt her nod, felt her hands clutch nervously at her back. "I'm sorry." She kissed her lightly on the cheek then pulled away. "I should have known Charlie would have a scanner, but I just didn't think."

Morgan moved away but kept a tight grip on her arm. "How bad is it?"

"Don't know yet. I'm waiting on fire and rescue from Gunnison." She glanced at her watch. "In this weather, they said to expect a good hour travel time."

"That's being generous. I would think an hour and a half, at least."

"Ed Wade is here. He saw it go down. Said he was behind Googan and Googan put his brakes on going around the curve and just went into a spin and right over the side. Hit black ice."

"Dear God," Morgan whispered.

"He called a buddy of his over at Thompson's Ranch. Mitch something or other. He's bringing a truck over with a winch."

"Mitch Hamilton. But a winch isn't going to bring Googan's truck up."

Reese shook her head. "No. For me to go down." She watched Morgan's eyes widen and she took her arm and led her out of the light, away from Ed's curious gaze. "It's the only option now, Morgan."

"You're going to tie onto the end of a rope and go over the side of Dead Man's Ridge? Then what? That canyon's two hundred feet deep."

"The truck's not all the way into the canyon. Ed estimates about a hundred and thirty feet."

"And the winch is what?"

She paused. "A hundred." She watched as Morgan's jaw set.

"I won't tell you how crazy that is. I know it's your job."

"Thank you."

"But you do know how this ridge got its name, right?"

"I think I can guess, yes."

Morgan surprised her by slipping into her arms again. "Please be careful," she said quietly. "I would miss you terribly."

Reese felt Morgan's lips trail across her cheek as she pulled out of her arms. She didn't know what to say. She just nodded, never taking her eyes from Morgan's. But now wasn't the time to contemplate the lips that had very nearly brushed her own.

She watched as Morgan made a careful turnaround and headed back down the mountain, then trudged back up the road to where Ed waited. He gave a half-smile, then motioned with his head to where Morgan had been.

"She's kinda special around here," he said.

"Yes."

"Everyone kinda looks after her."

Reese nodded.

"You're looking after her too, huh?"

Reese grinned. "Something like that." She walked back to the edge as full dark descended on them. In the distance she heard the whine of a truck.

"That'd be Mitch," Ed said.

"Great." She went to the back of her truck and opened up the toolbox, finding the thick rope they kept in there for pulling cars out of the snow. She tossed it at him. "You fish. You any good with knots?"

"Oh, sure. What do you need?"

"Some sort of harness for me. I don't want to be dangling off the side just clinging to a rope."

Ed nodded and walked into the glare of his truck headlights. "Sure, I can fix it up."

Reese walked to the middle of the road to wait, her mind alternating between Googan, who was most likely dead, and Morgan, whose frightened eyes and clinging arms had tugged at Reese's heart.

Damn.

"Slow, goddammit," Reese yelled up. "Is he trying to kill me?"

"My fault," Ed called down to her. "I didn't have the tension out."

She pushed off the rock wall, shining her flashlight down below. Googan's truck, while smashed to hell, was resting on its tires. Judging by the dents on the roof, she would guess it had flipped at least once. She looked back up to Ed, motioning him to lower her again. The makeshift harness they'd assembled was cutting into her thighs and back, but it felt tight.

Little by little, she was lowered into the canyon, the stinging cold of the ice pellets as they hit her face making her realize just how precarious the situation was. If Googan was still alive, no doubt hypothermia was setting in. And if his truck was smashed, the frame bent, they'd have a hell of a time getting him out.

She flashed her light around again, seeing the truck closer now. She could make out Googan, his body slumped over the steering wheel. She guessed they were about fifty feet away, and if the winch stopped now there were no footholds for her. No way could she reach him.

So as she slipped lower, she turned, flashing her light against the canyon wall, trying to find a tiny ledge where she could get a foothold, anything to support her while she got out of the harness. As luck would have it, the lip in the canyon that Googan's truck rested on was rocky and jagged. Her feet brushed a boulder now and Googan's truck was still a good thirty feet down.

She jerked as the winch stopped. She looked up, seeing Ed in the light, giving her a thumbs-up.

"That's it, Chief," he yelled down. "We'll keep it steady."

Easier said than done. She kicked off the wall, putting some swing in the rope, her momentum carrying her flush against the rock face. She held on, finding her footing. She tested the rock with her weight and it held. Pulling some slack in the rope, she fumbled with the knot at her waist, careful not to undo the slipknots Ed had made for the harness. Once free, she slid off the boulder, her boots landing with a quiet thud on the rock ledge.

Flashing the light around, she looked for the safest route down, then carefully made her way lower—slipping once on a snow-covered boulder and landing hard on her ass—toward Googan. She stopped as she slipped again, small rocks rolling off the ledge and she listened as they bounced down into the canyon.

She went around to the driver's side, closest to the canyon wall. The window was broken and she reached in, touching Googan's neck, feeling for a pulse. Her eyes widened in surprise as she felt a steady beat.

"Googan," she said loudly, squeezing his shoulder. He was still slumped over the steering wheel and she saw the blood on his face. "Googan, can you hear me?"

She stepped back, surveying the door. The roof was smashed, bending the doorframe. She pulled anyway, but it wouldn't budge.

"Googan, come on now," she said. "Wake up."

She stood on the running board, peering inside the truck. He had his seatbelt on, thankfully, and the air bags had deployed but were deflated. She flashed the light around then grimaced as the beam landed on his legs. One was bent grotesquely and blood had soaked his pant leg.

"Jesus," she whispered.

Reaching around him, she pulled his handheld radio out. "Ed, you copy?" She waited. "Ed, come in." She had given Ed her own radio, hoping to communicate.

There was a little static before Ed's voice came back. "Yeah, Chief. I can hear you."

"He's alive. Unconscious. Badly fractured leg, loss of blood. Laceration on his forehead. Copy?"

"Yeah, ten-four, Chief."

"I'll stay down here until Fire and Rescue gets here." She released the button then waited. Nothing. "You copy?"

"Yes. Sorry, Chief. I never learned how to use these radio things."

"I just didn't want you to pull the rope back up."

"Yes, ma'am."

Reese nodded, then flashed her light back to the rope, some thirty feet away. Radio transmission had a way of being twisted, and she hoped he hadn't thought she'd said *to* pull the rope back up. But it dangled lazily off the cliff, the breeze swaying it slightly. She whipped her head around when she heard Googan moan.

"Googan? Can you hear me?" She touched his face. It felt cold and clammy. She patted his cheek lightly. "Googan? Wake up, man."

His eyes fluttered opened, then closed again.

"Come on, stay with me. We'll get you out of here in no time."

"Chief?"

"Yeah. I'm here, Googan." She stuck her head through the window again. "I didn't want to move you. Can you sit back?"

He leaned back slowly, revealing the nasty gash across his forehead.

"Jesus, man."

"I can't feel my legs," he murmured.

"They're pinned under the dash. One's broken for sure. I can't see the other one." She pulled out of the truck and tried to open the toolbox on the back. It wouldn't budge. "Where's your first-aid kit?"

"I...I don't remember."

"Okay. I'm going to try to get the toolbox open. It's probably

157

in there."

"Don't leave me."

She paused. "I'm not. I'll be right here." She squeezed his shoulder, cursing herself for not thinking to bring her own first-aid kit down with her. But honestly, she had expected the worse. Yes, like Morgan said, this ridge got its name for a reason.

Opening the toolbox proved to be a lesson in patience. Reese could find nothing to pry it open, so she settled for two rocks. One, flat with a pointed edge that she placed against the toolbox's lid. The other, she used as a hammer. Eventually, the lid gave way and she was able to pull it open enough to see the black bag with large white letters: FIRST AID. She grabbed it and ripped it open, finding the large sterile bandages and some gauze and tape.

"Lean your head back, Googan. You've got a cut," she said as she tore small strips of tape. "Your head's split open."

"That could explain the headache," he mumbled.

She smiled briefly, then covered the wound, holding the bandage in place with one hand while taping the corners with the other, making it as tight as she dared. "It's not much," she said, "but maybe it'll help with the bleeding."

"How bad's my leg?"

"It looks bad. Compound fracture."

He rolled his head toward her, his eyes barely open. "That's the one where the bone breaks through the skin?"

She nodded.

"Bleeding?"

She nodded again. "Yeah."

His eyes slipped closed. "I'm sorry I was mean to you when you first got here."

She laughed quietly. "I wasn't exactly the queen of nice."

Silence for a moment, then he said, "How'd you get down here?"

"Mitch Hamilton brought a truck by with a winch."

"You're crazier than I thought," he murmured.

She shivered from the cold, the snow still gently falling

around them. *Yeah, crazy.* But it was her job. "You cold?"

"Don't know. Can't feel a whole lot."

"We'll get you out of here soon." *I hope.*

"Gunnison?"

"Yeah. Fire and rescue." She glanced at her watch. "They should be here any minute." The radio broke static then Ed Wade's voice sounded.

"Chief?"

"Yes, come back."

"We see the lights coming."

"Wonderful. Tell them they're going to need torches. The door is jammed."

"Ten-four, Chief."

Reese chuckled. "Good job, Ed."

"Thank you. Is Googan conscious yet?"

"Yeah. I told him you were going to take over his job, you're getting so good with this radio stuff."

"Ten-four."

"How'd you find Ed?" Googan asked.

"He was behind you on the road. He saw it happen." She squeezed his shoulder. "You're damn lucky someone saw it go down." She looked up when she saw the emergency lights flashing across the canyon. "Rescue is here," she said. "Won't be long now."

"Thank you for staying with me."

"Don't thank me, Googan. You'd have done the same for me, right?"

He smiled. "Sure. Do you think you could call my mother?"

"Of course."

"She lives in Gunnison now. Eloise has her number."

"I'll call her. I'll have her meet you at the hospital, how's that?"

"That'd be good," he said, his voice low.

She patted his shoulder as his eyes slipped closed again, but his breathing was even and steady. She looked up to the canyon rim, seeing two dark figures as they began their rappel down.

CHAPTER THIRTY

Morgan stared into the fire, absently shaking her glass, hearing the ice tinkling the sides, the shot of scotch long gone. She hoped Reese wouldn't mind, but she'd found the bottle of scotch, still unopened. And she needed something to calm her nerves.

Not that the alcohol had done much to reduce her anxiety, she noted as she placed the glass on the mantel. So here she waited, at Reese's cabin, fearing for Googan's life, fearing for Reese's safety. Even though she told herself it was silly to worry, that it was Reese's job, that she was plenty capable…still, she worried. And that was disturbing in itself. They weren't a couple. They weren't in a relationship. Yet she had ignored common sense and driven up the mountain to make sure it wasn't Reese who had plunged off the side. And here she was, waiting at Reese's place, waiting as if she had a *right* to wait for her.

"It's just sex. Just sex," she said. *Nothing more.*

But it was starting to feel like more. Barely a month into this...this *arrangement* and she was already having a hard time keeping it in the context it was meant to be. No strings, no commitments, no nothing. Just sex.

The slamming of a truck door brought her around and she glanced up just as Reese opened the door. Their eyes met across the room and Reese gave her a half-smile.

"I'm really glad you're here."

Morgan swallowed hard, curbing the impulse to fling herself into Reese's arms. She watched silently as Reese stomped her boots on the mat and shook the snow off her coat before hanging it up. But when Reese stepped into the room, the light showing the stress on her face, Morgan gave in to her instinct and walked across the room, wrapping both arms around Reese. Reese held her tight, burying her face in Morgan's neck.

"He's alive," Reese said. "A miracle, but it looks like his truck flipped once and landed upright."

Morgan pulled away slightly. "How bad?"

"Badly broken leg. Compound fracture in two places. His head was split open on his forehead, but he was conscious." Reese went to the fire and held her hands out to the warmth. She spotted the empty glass. "Found my scotch, huh?"

"I hope you don't mind."

"Actually, I'd love some myself."

"Let me get it for you."

"Morgan?"

Morgan turned, meeting her gaze.

"About you coming out there tonight—"

"I'm sorry, Reese. I know I shouldn't have—"

"No, no. It was...it was nice. I'm not used to anyone being worried about me."

"I panicked. I—"

"It felt good, Morgan. I felt like, well, it's been forever since I've felt like I was a part of something, of someone...like I mattered. And when I saw you, saw the fear in your eyes...it meant a lot."

Morgan felt her defenses slip at Reese's words, felt the tiny stirrings of her heart. She moved closer, curling her hand behind Reese's neck and pulling her close, meeting her lips for the very first time. Their kiss was gentle, exploring, and she let Reese pull her into her arms, her mouth opening, her tongue shyly meeting Reese's, moaning as Reese's hands slipped to her hips and brought their bodies flush together.

Forgotten was the scotch, forgotten was her no kissing rule. They stood there for what seemed like hours, just kissing... touching. But their passion for each other soon demanded to be heard, and Reese lowered her to the rug, the fire burning hotly as her hand slipped inside Morgan's jeans, Reese's mouth never once leaving hers.

Morgan came almost instantly and she clung to Reese, no longer fearing for Reese's safety, but fearing for her own heart instead.

CHAPTER THIRTY-ONE

"Do you know how long it's been since I spent Christmas with someone?" Reese asked as she stole a piece of turkey from the platter where Morgan was still carving the giant bird.

"If you keep nibbling, you won't be hungry for dinner."

"But it's so good. The last time I had turkey with stuffing, my dad was still alive."

"Dressing. Turkey and *dressing*," Morgan corrected. "Traditional southern style cornbread dressing."

Reese leaned closer and kissed her lightly on the lips. "Whatever it is, it smells fabulous." Reese grabbed her cell phone from the counter. "I'm going to check in with Carlton, make sure everything's quiet," she said.

Morgan stared at her retreating back, smiling at Reese's concern over the sheriff's office. With Googan out for at least three months, Reese was forced to hire Carlton back on. She'd told him his job was that of traffic cop, nothing more, but she checked up on him constantly.

She went back to her turkey, thinking of the quick kiss Reese had given her. Since the night of Googan's accident, things had changed between them. It was her fault, she knew. If she just hadn't given in to that basic instinct to kiss, maybe things would be as they were. But no. The intensity of their lovemaking went to nearly unbearable heights with the addition of kissing. Yes, it was more intimate. It was more *real*. The looks they now shared held a deeper tie than just between lovers. Yes, they were lovers. But they'd also grown to care about each other.

So yes, things had changed between them. They both knew it, yet neither mentioned the shift in their relationship. Changes, yes. But still the same. Reese was still leaving in November. That had not changed.

Morgan sighed, wondering how she was going to stop herself from falling in love with the woman.

Reese folded her phone, satisfied Carlton was doing nothing more than playing solitaire on Eloise's computer. All was quiet. As it should be on this snowy Christmas Day. She couldn't imagine it being any more complete. Light snow falling, making everything postcard perfect, the smells of Christmas dinner filling the cabin, and a beautiful woman to share it with.

Reese went to the large picture window and stared out, feeling contentment she hadn't felt in her adult life. And it was certainly not something she ever expected to find here in this lonely little town.

Yet lonely was the furthest thing from her mind when dawn woke them this morning. Morgan was snuggled close, her arm wrapped around Reese's waist. And Reese had held her, her fingers moving lazily across her skin, feeling the stirrings of desire from even such a simple act. But it was enough. And when Morgan lifted her head, seeking her lips, Reese was there, rolling them over, touching Morgan everywhere, starving for her as if it were the first time, bringing Morgan to orgasm as her lips suckled her breast.

She closed her eyes, remembering how Morgan had called her name as she climaxed, remembering how Morgan had reciprocated, had boldly spread her legs and made love to her with her mouth.

January was right around the corner. By April, everyone would be gearing up for summer, and by May, the tourists would start flocking to the area. Morgan would be busy during the summer, working nearly every day. Then fall and hunting season.

And then November would roll around. November was election time. And November meant freedom. A new interim sheriff would be named and she would be free to go, free to leave this tiny little town that she so despised when she first got here.

She sighed. The thought of leaving here just didn't hold the same elation it once had. Leaving here meant leaving Morgan.

So much for her well concocted plan that they could spend the year having sex and remain unattached emotionally. What had she been thinking?

Well, she'd thought that they would get together a few times a month, have sex, then go their separate ways. She never dreamed that she'd want to have Morgan in her bed every night, whether they made love or not. She never dreamed that Morgan would want her company on a daily basis as well. And of course, she never dreamed that the sex would be this great.

"Hey."

She turned, finding Morgan watching her.

"You okay?"

Reese nodded. "Yeah. Just thinking."

She turned back to the window and felt Morgan move closer. Her eyes closed as Morgan slipped her arms around her from behind, resting her head on Reese's shoulder.

"It's beautiful, isn't it?"

Reese smiled. "I thought you hated the snow."

"Not on Christmas. You can't hate the snow on Christmas."

Reese turned and faced her, pulling Morgan into her arms. She felt Morgan's lips nuzzle her neck and she waited, feeling

Morgan's mouth move across her face, finally to her lips. A slow, tender kiss, lips on lips, just the barest touch of tongue.

"I love kissing you," Reese murmured.

"Mmmm."

And just like that, their kisses grew bolder, more demanding, and the fire was started between them. And as often occurred, they didn't make it to the bedroom, being satisfied with the rug in front of the fireplace. Their clothing slowly disappeared, hands and mouths taking its place against their skin.

CHAPTER THIRTY-TWO

"It's April," Morgan said dramatically as she pointed out the window, "and there's a freakin' blizzard blowing in." She stared at Tina. "Can you believe that?"

"Oh, my God. Like it's the first blizzard we've ever had in April."

Morgan sighed in frustration as she huffed back to her desk. "I want to see the ground. I want to see a damn flower. I want to see some *green*. Is that too much to ask?"

"I see someone's got spring fever," Tina said. "Isn't it enough to have me back in the office? Must you have sunshine too?" she teased.

"And how exactly did you talk Charlie into hiring you back early?"

"I told him I had cabin fever so bad that I was having dreams of hacking up my family with an ax."

Morgan laughed. "And he bought that? Isn't that what you

used last year?"

"No. Last year I threatened to go postal and shoot up Sloan's Bar."

"Oh, that's right. And he made the mistake of telling Sloan."

"Speaking of telling, when are you going to spill it about you and the Chief?"

Morgan felt her face flush. "I don't know what you mean."

"Give me a break. This we're *just friends* crap has got to stop. My sources tell me your truck hasn't been at your house in months."

"Your source, little miss busybody Tracy, is wrong. I am often at my house in the evenings," Morgan lied. Truth was, she hadn't slept at her own house since January. But she *did* still go to her house for a change of clothes. It wasn't like she was living with Reese or anything.

"I just want to know why all the secrecy? So you're seeing each other? The whole town knows. Why do you insist you're not?"

"Because the whole town doesn't need to know everything, that's why." She met Tina's gaze. "Yes, we're seeing each other," she said. There was really no sense in continuing the charade. "For a few more months, anyway." She was surprised how those words stung.

"What do you mean?"

"She's only here until November."

"Oh. So what? This is like killing time?"

"God, that sounds so cheap when you say it like that. But yeah. I suppose." She didn't feel the need to tell Tina about their *arrangement*.

"Well, I guess there are worse ways to spend the winter." Tina grinned. "I bet she's good in bed."

"No, no, no. I will not go there with you."

"Come on. You finally have a sex life and you won't share?"

Morgan hesitated. Part of her wanted to confess to Tina that she thought she was in over her head with Reese. But she thought better of it. She really wasn't up to going over all of the rules of their relationship, and how she was on the verge of breaking every one of them. So she gave in. A little.

"The sex is beyond fabulous," she admitted with a grin. "It's the best sex I've ever had in my life. In fact—"

"You don't have to rub it in."

"You asked."

It was still snowing when Morgan drove to Reese's cabin late that afternoon. It was the kind of snow where the clouds hung low, blocking out the mountains, bringing a heaviness to everything around. The branches of the spruce trees were laden with snow, straining to keep their shape as they drooped to the ground.

She hated spring snowstorms. *Hated* them. Just when you thought things were beginning to thaw. Just when the ice was starting to break on Lake San Cristobal. Just when there'd been nearly a week of sunshine, the streets in town finally snow free, *this* happens. Snow, snow and more snow. And she knew if it weren't for Reese keeping her occupied, she'd have snapped by now.

But she was pleasantly surprised to see smoke twirling out of the chimney and Reese's truck parked out front. Reese hadn't beaten her home in a long time. She paused. *Home.* Yeah, it felt like home here. Amazing, but it did. She had her tiny house in town where she and Jackson had lived for seven years, yet Ron Brightmen's hunting cabin felt like home. Whether it was because Jackson wasn't there anymore or because Reese was here, she didn't know.

Reese was adding another log to the fire when she walked in, and she hung her coat beside Reese's on the rack.

"Still coming down pretty good, huh?"

"Damn April storm," Morgan muttered as she joined Reese by the fire.

Reese laughed. "Yeah, I knew you'd be cranky."

"It's supposed to be spring."

"It's barely April."

"It's mid-April," Morgan corrected, then covered Reese's mouth with her hand when she would have spoken again. She felt Reese's tongue wet her palm and she pulled away smiling. "What do I smell?"

"Dinner."

Morgan raised an eyebrow. "*You* cooked dinner?"

"Of course not. But I didn't think you'd be in any mood to, so I stopped by Sloan's for the famous double-battered fried chicken."

Morgan leaned closer and kissed Reese. "That was very sweet of you."

"Tracy said she missed you, by the way."

Morgan rolled her eyes. "I saw her at lunch."

"Well, you know, maybe we could go by there occasionally for a beer and burger, like we used to."

"You mean, seeing as how the whole town knows about this affair anyway?"

Reese smiled. "Yeah, that. You don't mind, do you?"

"No, I guess I don't. I don't know why I thought we could keep it a secret anyway." She didn't mention Tina's definition of their affair as *just killing time*. She didn't want to think about that.

"Oh, did you know Lou's Grocery rents DVDs?"

Morgan laughed. "Yes, but what were you doing at Lou's?"

"Before the fried chicken idea, I thought I might surprise you and cook dinner." She grinned. "However, I quickly saw that I was overambitious. He did have frozen pizza though. I nearly got that."

Morgan was touched by Reese's thoughtfulness. And surprised at how quickly Reese had gotten to know her moods. No, cooking dinner was the last thing she wanted to do after brooding over the snowstorm all day. She thanked her with a lingering kiss on the mouth, but pulled away when Reese's hands slid up to her breasts.

"I'm starving," she said with a smile. "You'll have to wait."

Much later—after dinner and after bed—after Reese had made love to her so thoroughly, Morgan lay awake, relishing the feel of Reese's arm across her waist, the soft breath caressing her skin, the involuntary twitching of Reese's hand as she slept. All things Morgan had grown to love, and all things she knew she was going to miss when Reese walked out of her life. Six more months. That's all she would have. Six more months. And then they would say their goodbyes and go about their own lives, and all of this would be just a fond memory to look back on.

She told herself she wouldn't fall in love with Reese. She told herself to just enjoy the sex and be done with it. And yes, she did enjoy the sex. As she'd told Tina, it was the best she'd ever had. They were so attuned to each other's needs, each other's desires, that their lovemaking was nearly effortless, two people giving and receiving pleasure as naturally as could be. But it had long ceased being just sex. They made love. It was in the way they looked at each other, the way they touched, the way they kissed.

She wondered how difficult it would be for Reese to leave come November. Would it hurt her as much? Would her heart ache as Morgan knew hers no doubt would? Or would she be able to separate it all and remember that what they shared was a no strings sexual arrangement? Nothing more, nothing less. Would Reese be able to do that?

Morgan closed her eyes, her heart heavy on this cold, snowy April night. She turned her head, her lips brushing across Reese's face. She felt Reese's arm tighten around her and she smiled. Yes, one of the many things she would miss.

CHAPTER THIRTY-THREE

"My, God, it's the sun," Morgan said sarcastically two days later as it finally peeked out, the snow clouds—at last—moving on.

"Yeah, crazy weather," Charlie said. "We're going to be in the fifties tomorrow and in the sixties on Friday."

Morgan stared at him. "That's not good." As much as she wanted spring to get here, that was too warm too fast. Especially after the high country just got five feet of fresh snow.

"I know. Ripe for avalanches. We should probably post the warning signs at the trailheads. After all this snow, I'd guess we'll have a few skiers head up to our mountains here."

"Probably should close Cutter's Ridge too. At least at the top. The back side of the mountain, besides Cutter's Chute, has what? Four or five other avalanche chutes?"

"I say five, even though those yahoos in the department claim only four meet the criteria."

"We want to put the red flag up?"

"Yeah. Let's hold off on the black until we hear something."

And it didn't take long. Within minutes, reports were coming in of avalanches running all across the state, the most severe in Aspen where a massive fall had covered the road, burying three cars. The recommendation for black flag warnings on all susceptible trails had come.

Morgan scrambled to find the signs they hadn't had to use in two years. Berta insisted she'd put them in the storage shed in the back, but after fifteen minutes of searching, Morgan couldn't find them. She trudged back through the snow and into the back room to tell her as much.

"I don't know what you did with them then," Berta said. "That's where I put them."

Morgan put her hands on her hips. "Do you *mind* helping me look, Berta? This is kinda important," she said impatiently.

"Maybe Tina put them somewhere. You know how she's always cleaning up."

"Then do you mind calling her?"

Morgan went into the supply closet where she knew where the flags were, at least. Only twice had she had to put up the black flags. The red warning went up nearly every year for Cutter's Ridge, even though *technically* Cutter's Chute was on private property. The other four active chutes that were near trails were all on public land. And the one that wasn't officially recognized— Cinnamon Chute as the locals called it—dumped its load yearly on the Alpine Loop.

"Tina said she put them in here," Berta said as she stuck her head inside.

"In *here*?" Morgan turned around, looking between the bookcase and the wall, the only place the signs would fit. And sure enough, there they were. "So all of our other signs are kept out in the storage shed," she said, "but Tina felt the need to keep these in here?" She shook her head. Tina had a tendency to clean and tidy up the place when she was bored. And inevitably she would put something in an odd place and they could never find it. Paul claimed she did the same thing at home. "Tell her to keep her grubby hands off my signs," Morgan said as she brushed past Berta, signs tucked under her arm.

The drive to the trailhead was made with her window open, and Morgan couldn't believe how warm it had gotten in the last hour. But it happened sometimes when late season fronts dumped snow then stalled over the plains, only to back up as a warm front pulling in tropical breezes from the Gulf. The avalanche danger was high, sure, but the prospect of hitting sixty tomorrow had her nearly giddy. Spring—*real* spring—was right around the corner. She could feel it. Oh, they'd still get the occasional dusting of snow, but it would be gone by midday.

"God, I love it," she said as she stood on the trailhead, taking a deep breath of the cool mountain air, so pure it nearly hurt her lungs. She turned a circle, enjoying the quiet, listening to nothing except the occasional call of a nuthatch as it fought through the snow to reach the branches of the trees to forage for seeds.

She pulled one of the TRAIL CLOSED signs from the truck and got her hammer and went about finding a spot to put it. The snow was deep, so she used her boots to scrape back enough to find solid ground. She wasn't too worried about the sign though. It would only be up for a couple of days. If the avalanche chutes were going to run—and with this warm weather she had no doubt they would—they'd drop their load of snow within twenty-four hours.

She was just driving away when her cell rang. She slowed as she rounded the corner onto the forest road, her tires slipping on the snow. "Hey, Charlie, what's up?"

"Cinnamon Chute just ran," he said. "Got a call from the road crew. Damn near buried a snowplow."

"What were they doing up on the Alpine Loop anyway?"

"Oh, you know Brightmen's got connections. He's probably worried all this snow will cut into his Jeep rentals."

Morgan rolled her eyes. "He's got another six weeks before he can even *think* about his Jeep tours. Good grief."

"Yeah, well, just wanted to let you know. And I put a call in to the lodge, but Ellen said they wouldn't have any guests until Friday. The danger should be past by then."

"Okay, Charlie. I'm heading back in. See you in a bit."

She stopped when the forest road met the highway, looking out over the snow-white mountains. It was almost surreal, all this white. Every tree, every rock, every spot of ground was buried in snow. The bright sunshine and deep blue skies were a sharp contrast to the land covered in white. But with the window down, she could hear the drip, drip, drip of snow as it melted. If it did indeed get into the sixties by Friday, all this would be gone from the trees, melted away as if it never happened.

And then the snowmelt would fill the streams, dumping into Henson Creek and Hines Creek, and others on its way to the Gunnison River. And Ed Wade would be a happy man when the fly fishermen descended on them, hoping to land that monster trout.

She smiled as she looked toward the valley of Lake City, picturing the warm sunny days of summer when winter would be just a memory. But she wanted this day to be a memory too. So she fished in her backpack for her small digital camera. She stood on the road in front of her truck, snapping a few pictures to add to her ever-growing file.

She heard the distant rumble just as she was about to get back into her truck. She tilted her head, listening, then grabbed the door handle as the ground literally shook, a deafening roar replaced the peaceful quiet, sending the noisy jays scurrying for cover.

"Wow," she murmured as she fumbled for her cell. "Wow, wow, wow." Her fingers trembled as she called Charlie. He answered right away. "Did you hear it?" she asked excitedly. "Felt like a damn earthquake."

"Cutter's Chute?"

"Yeah. That didn't take long. With all that snow, I figured it wouldn't run until tomorrow."

"Are you on the highway yet?"

"Just there." She grinned. "Man, that was awesome. Makes

me want to strap on skis just to go take a look."

"Yeah. I hope Johnnie wasn't out and about."

"He knows better. Besides, all this snow, his cabin is probably buried."

"Okay, I'll report the run. Be careful on your way back."

But instead of heading back to town, Morgan called the lodge. She had no doubt they'd heard the run, but just as a precaution, she thought she'd check in with them. Even if they had no guests coming until Friday, their main route into the forest was now cut off by the avalanche. It had been four years since Cutter's Chute had dropped its load. Finding a new path into the forest wasn't normally a concern for Rick.

"Hi, Ellen. It's Morgan. I guess you heard the roar, huh?"

"My, God, yes. It scared the crap out of me. I'm here alone and the whole place was shaking."

"Where are the guys?"

"Oh, since things were quiet around here, they took their skis and went on an early hike."

"There? Up above the lodge? Ellen—"

"Now, Morgan, Rick's got more sense than to try to ski Cutter's Chute."

"Yeah, but what trail did they take?" Morgan pulled away, driving toward the lodge instead of town. "Why don't you call his cell?"

"He doesn't take his phone. There's no service back there. You know that."

"Okay, well, you don't sound worried, but I'm on my way there. I'd just feel better if I knew they didn't take the ridge trail, that's all."

"Oh, Morgan, you don't have to—"

"I'll be there in a few minutes," she said, ending the call. She had a bad feeling. A real bad feeling. So she called Reese.

"Where are you?" Reese asked as soon as she answered.

"On my way to the lodge."

"Be careful, Morgan. There's avalanches and snowslides all over the place. Half the mountain came down on the highway going to Gunnison, and Thompson's Ranch called and said they had a snowslide leading up the pass and that road is buried." She gave a heavy sigh. "Googan's not fit to drive yet so I've got Carlton helping me close roads."

Morgan glanced at the sheer wall of rock and snow as she drove past, speeding up as much as she dared in the slush. No doubt this would give way any minute. "I was up here when Cutter's Chute ran. It shook my truck. I'm surprised the road is still open to the lodge, but the snow is still clinging here."

"What are you doing at the lodge anyway?"

"Ellen said Rick and Kenny were out on skis."

"What the hell?"

"I know. But Ellen doesn't seem to think they took the trail to the ridge. I just want to make sure."

"No, Morgan. You're not going out there. The mountains aren't stable."

"I'm not going *out there*, Reese. I just want to see what trail they took. If they went into the valley, they're fine. But if they took the trail to the ridge, it's right in the path. I'm trying not to panic, but—"

"Morgan, listen to me. I've got enough to worry about without you going out in this mess. Please don't do anything stupid."

"Oh? You mean like tying on to a winch and letting myself get dropped into Dead Man's Canyon during a snowstorm? Stupid like that?"

"Funny, *Zula*."

Morgan smiled. "I'll be in touch *Clarice*."

She heard Reese's quiet laughter as she disconnected. She never thought the day would come that she'd actually enjoy being called *Zula*. But somehow, when Reese said it, it gave her a warm, tingly feeling. It had become an endearment that was known only to them, and they used it on occasion, as lovers often do.

CHAPTER THIRTY-FOUR

Reese was still smiling as she rounded a corner heading south down Hines Creek Road, but the smile soon faded as she came upon a snow bank blocking the road. She slammed on her brakes, the four-wheel drive holding as the truck came to a stop without skidding. She looked out her window up above where the road had been cut into the mountainside. Heavy snow like this last storm just dumped on them had to go somewhere. She backed up, looking for a spot to turn around, hoping she wouldn't have to back all the way down the mountain road.

"Carlton, come in," she said into her radio.

"Here, Chief."

"Hines Creek Road has a snowslide. Have they cleared the highway going to Gunnison yet?"

"Ten-four. Just about done."

"Okay. Let them know about this one." She stopped as she backed into a narrow turnout. "I'm going to head up to

Slumgullion."

"Ten-four, Chief."

Reese rolled her eyes as she put the radio down. She never thought she'd say this, but she missed Googan. And it'd be at least another six weeks before he was ready to come back. Even after two surgeries on his leg, he'd still most likely walk with a limp the rest of his life. But as Googan liked to say, beats being dead.

As she headed up the pass to the Slumgullion slide, she called Morgan. By the sound of her labored breathing, Reese knew she was out on skis.

"Morgan, what the hell are you doing?"

"I'm glad you called. Their tracks lead to the ridge trail, not the valley."

"Shit. Okay. Do not—and I mean it—do *not* attempt to go after them."

"Reese, I'm just going—"

"Goddammit, no you're not," she said loudly. "You let me call search and rescue."

"There are avalanches all over the state. How the hell are you going to get a crew out here?"

"Then I'll get fire and rescue in Gunnison. They've got a chopper."

Morgan took a deep breath. "He's my friend," she said quietly. "And Ellen still thinks they went to the valley. I have to tell her."

"I know, Morgan. And I'm on my way there right now. But you've got to let the experts do this. No offense, but you're not trained." She heard the sigh, heard Morgan clear her throat, no doubt fighting back tears. "Morgan, I'm ten minutes away. Meet me at the lodge." She paused. "Please?"

"I know. You're right."

"Good. Now let me call it in. Why don't you get in touch with Tina? See if she can come out."

"Yeah, I will. She and Ellen are good friends."

"Okay. Be right there." Reese didn't wait for a reply as she disconnected, then searched her phone for another number.

§

By the time Morgan hung up with Tina, they had both worked themselves into near hysteria. Tina was on her way over. And now as she took off her skis and plunged them into a snow bank, she had the task of telling Ellen. Of course, she could hide out and wait for Reese. But Ellen didn't really know Reese. News like this was best heard coming from a friend.

Really, there was no news. For all they knew, Rick and Kenny had already crossed the path of the avalanche run and were safely on the other side when it dropped. Safe but stuck. With all this snow, no way could they bushwhack up the mountain, and the trail they needed to take up the ridge would have been buried in the run. But it was a much better thought than them getting caught in the avalanche.

She saw Ellen come out of the lodge and knew she would have no reprieve. Best to just get it over with. So she shook her head, meeting Ellen's eyes head on. "They took Ridge Trail," she said.

"Oh, God, no."

"I've already called Chief Daniels. She's calling in a search team."

Ellen's eyes widened.

"Do not panic, Ellen. They could have made it across the path before it ran. They could have already been up the trail enough to be out of harm's way."

"Or they could be buried." Ellen turned away, her shoulders shaking as she tried to control herself.

Morgan walked behind her and turned her around, pulling her into a tight hug. "They'll bring a helicopter. We'll be able to spot them," she said. "I called Tina. She's on her way over. She'll stay with you. I'll need to assist them with coordinates."

Ellen nodded. "I know. And you're right. I shouldn't panic." She pulled away and wiped at her eyes. "Why do we always think the worst at times like this?"

Morgan shrugged. "It's just what we do."

"Well, I'm not going to think the worst. Rick is experienced. He would never take a chance with Cutter's Chute, not after all the snow we got. He would know better."

"Yes, I think so."

"Maybe they were just going to go down the canyon to the river."

"Maybe so." Although she knew better. The canyon was too steep for skiing. They'd have to go farther up the ridge before they'd be able to ski down the canyon. And that meant crossing Cutter's Chute.

"Thanks, Morgan. You're a good friend. Now I think I'll do what I do best and that's busy myself in the kitchen." She stared at Morgan. "I think they're fine. Don't you?"

Morgan thought no such thing. She was a worrier from way back and usually overreacted. Why else would she drive through ice and snow up Dead Man's Ridge to check on Reese? But she couldn't tell Ellen that. So she nodded. "I think they're just fine."

Reese adjusted her headset, watching as Morgan held on tightly when the helicopter banked right.

"Over the ridge, we should be able to see the run on the left," Morgan said.

But as they topped the ridge a gust of wind caught them, and Reese felt herself being lifted out of her seat.

"Hang on," the pilot said tersely in their headsets. He steadied the craft, then took them lower toward Cutter's Chute.

"Oh, my God," Morgan said. "This is the first time I've seen the run from the air."

"It's huge," Reese said, but another wind gust tossed them off course again.

"Look quick," the pilot said. "It's too windy for another pass."

"But—"

"No, ma'am," he said to Morgan. "I can't put more lives in

danger. It's too windy to keep her up."

Reese reached out and squeezed Morgan's arm. Truth be told, they probably shouldn't have even attempted the one pass over the site. There was nothing but white below them as they flew across the avalanche run and topped the mountain, heading back toward the lodge.

"The wind will be calm in the morning," he said. "If you think you can find us a place to stay tonight, we'll make another pass at daybreak."

"I'm certain Ellen can put you up at the lodge," Reese said.

They were back on the ground within minutes, and Tina and Ellen stood at the steps to the lodge, waiting.

"I'll tell them," Reese offered as she hopped out first.

"Thank you."

But she didn't have to say anything. Ellen knew.

"It's too windy to fly, right?"

"Right. We were able to make one pass over the run, that's it. They said they'll go out again at daybreak."

Ellen nodded. "Okay. Well, good thing we've got rooms." She squared her shoulders. "I've got a thick beef stew simmering. You and Morgan can stay for dinner too, Reese. There's plenty."

As she walked away, Reese turned to Tina. "In denial? What?"

"Partly, yes. And partly because she said she didn't *feel* like they were in trouble." Tina shrugged. "Everyone's got their own way of coping." She motioned to Morgan who walked over with the two crew members. "How is she?"

"Worried."

"Yeah. That's about all we can do, isn't it?"

Reese nodded. "Afraid so."

Dinner was a mostly quiet affair with Tina trying to force conversation among them. Ellen, for her part, at least pretended that everything was fine, telling Jonathan and Matt—the two crew members from Gunnison's Fire and Rescue—stories about some of their more daring guests who'd tried to snowmobile down Cutter's Chute.

182

Morgan sat quietly beside her, saying little, and Reese recognized the worry in her eyes. This was Morgan's town. These were her people. She loved and cared about them. It was something Reese wasn't used to. After leaving Vegas, she'd hopped around tourist towns, never staying too long in one place, never learning to truly *care* about the people there. She was just doing a job. But now she envied the closeness that Morgan had with Ellen and Tina, two people she'd only met since getting transferred here. Two people she let into her life. Not like Reese, who kept everyone at a distance. No wonder, even after six months, she still felt like an outsider. As Morgan had told her once, it was easier for her to cut and run if she didn't get involved in their lives.

All but Morgan. Try as she may, she couldn't say she was *not* involved with Morgan. She was. Right now, at this very minute, Morgan was the most important thing in her life.

And that scared the hell out of her.

She smiled slightly when she felt a light touch upon her thigh and Morgan's fingers gently squeezing. She looked across the table, finding Tina's eyes on them. She didn't care. She reached under the table and covered Morgan's hand, holding it tightly against her leg.

The loud ringing of the phone in the kitchen stopped Ellen in mid-sentence and she nearly ran for it. They all listened intently as Ellen's voice got louder.

"What? Johnnie? I can barely hear you."

"Johnnie Cutter," Morgan said to Reese.

Ellen came back in, the phone still to her ear, her eyes wide. "Oh, my God." Reese jumped up, taking the phone from Ellen. Ellen nearly fell into Tina's arms. "They're alive. He said they were alive."

Reese felt a wave of relief. "This is Reese Daniels," she said into the phone.

"Who?"

"The no-good lady sheriff," she said, grinning at Morgan who was listening.

"Oh, Chief Daniels. Yeah. This is Johnnie. I barely got a

signal on this fancy cell phone. Can you hear me?"

"I can hear you. Where are you?"

"I had to hike to the top of the damn mountain to get a signal. I'm standing in waist-deep snow, that's where the hell I am."

"What about Rick and Kenny?"

"The kid's got a broken leg, the best I can tell. The damn fools were at the base of the chute when it ran. They skied over the top of the canyon to beat it, probably fell twenty or thirty feet. I went down to check on things after I heard the run. I heard somebody hollering for help."

"Damn, Johnnie. You did good."

"Yeah, well we had a hell of a time getting the boy out. He can't put any weight on his left leg."

"Where are they now?"

"Oh, I imagine they're by the fire in my cabin. But he knew everyone would be worried so I hiked up. And who was the damn fool flying a helicopter in this wind? I thought I was going to have to do another rescue the way it was bouncing around up there."

Reese laughed. "That'd have been me and Morgan, with a crew from Gunnison."

"And she calls me an old crazy fool." He laughed. "The wind will calm down by morning. Have those fellas swing by with their chopper. There's an open space on the back side of the mountain. Morgan will know where it is. We'll put together a sled or something for the boy."

"I'll let everyone know. Thanks, Johnnie. We'll be around in the morning."

Ellen grabbed her arm as soon as she hung up. "Well, what did he say? How are they?"

"They're in his cabin. He thinks Kenny has a broken leg. That's the only injury he mentioned."

"How? I mean—"

"As Johnnie put it, the damn fools were at the base of the chute when it ran. He said they had to ski into the canyon."

"It's too steep there to ski," Morgan said.

"Yeah. That was the problem. He said it was a twenty-or thirty-foot drop."

"Oh, God," Ellen said. "It could have been so much worse."

Reese looked at Morgan. "He said there was a clearing on the back side of the mountain. They're going to ski there tomorrow and have the helicopter pick them up. You know what he's talking about?"

"Yes. It's essentially a boulder field, no vegetation. With this much snow, they should be able to ski it easily. But what about Kenny?"

"He said they would put him on a sled or something." She glanced at Jonathan and Matt who were listening. "That okay?"

They nodded. "That's great news," Matt said. "Sure, we can pick them up."

"I don't know how to thank you all," Ellen said, her eyes misting with tears again. "It could have been so tragic. Those two are my life. I don't know how I could have coped if I'd lost them."

"I thought you weren't worried," Tina teased.

"I lied," she said as tears and laughter came at the same time.

CHAPTER THIRTY-FIVE

Reese stood on the sidewalk as the warm breeze blew around them, staring at the sign. TONI'S HAIR AFFAIR. She glanced at Morgan.

"You're the one who didn't want Stella," Morgan reminded her.

Yes, that was true. The week before, as they sat outside in lawn chairs waiting for the charcoal to heat, Morgan had reached over and ruffled her hair. "You need a haircut."

Reese had tried to tame it. "I know. It's never been this long."

"Why don't you go see Stella?"

"Oh, no. She's a hundred years old. The one time I went, she used a curling iron and threatened to tease it if I didn't let her *pouf up the back*, as she called it."

And so here they stood on the main street in Gunnison, combining a grocery shopping trip with Reese's haircut.

"Go on in," Morgan said. "I'll just window shop." She glanced down the street. "Everyone's getting ready for tourist season. Can't you just feel it?"

"Yeah. A few more weeks." She pointed at the shop. "I'll find you when I'm done."

Morgan laughed and held up her cell phone. "Don't hunt for me too long."

Reese grinned. "I guess it would be easier to just call you." She paused at the door. "Have fun. Shouldn't take me long."

But when she saw the crowded shop, the ladies all talking at once, she was glad they'd had the foresight to make an appointment. She looked at the smiling girl at the counter. "I'm Reese Daniels," she said.

"Welcome, Reese. Try and find a seat. It'll just be a few minutes."

Reese looked back at the waiting room, seeing every seat occupied by someone's grandmother. *Lovely.* Everyone over the age of seventy must have an appointment this morning, she thought. But she didn't have to wait long. A woman, not much younger than old Stella in Lake City called for her.

"You must be new in town, hon," she said as she led Reese to a chair and immediately plunged both hands into Reese's hair. "Nice, thick hair. Very healthy. Just need a trim?"

Reese met her eyes in the mirror. "Looking more for the summer cut," she said. "I don't normally keep it this long."

"Well, not knowing how you normally wear it, would you like to look at some pictures in a magazine?"

"No," Reese said quickly. "Definitely not." She looked from side to side, then back to the woman in the mirror. "Look, I'm not really a big hair person. It's not that big a deal to me. Just kinda clean it up a little."

The woman lifted her hair. "Over the ears?"

"Not quite that short."

"Bangs?"

"God, no."

The woman spun the chair around and messed with the top.

187

"Too curly for bangs anyway."

"I don't have curly hair."

She smiled. "Hon, if this ain't curly, I don't know what is."

Reese narrowed her eyes. "Just cut it."

"Well, I'll do my best, but I don't want any complaining from you."

"No, ma'am."

And out came the bottle of water, the woman spraying her hair to wet it, her fingers moving through it as she shook her head in disapproval.

"What?"

"Such nice thick hair and you want to cut it off."

Reese gritted her teeth. She should have just gone to Stella. But the woman made quick work, her scissors snapping as her dark hair fell to her shoulders and gathered on the plastic cape before slipping to the floor. But as she watched, it got shorter and shorter. As the woman snipped above her ear, Reese arched an eyebrow.

"You have such a pretty face. Nice strong jawline. I felt shorter was the way to go," she said.

"Uh-huh."

She unsnapped the cape and shook the hair to the floor. "Time for a shampoo and blow-dry."

"That's not really necessary," Reese said as she got out of the chair.

"Of course it is. You have tiny hairs all over you."

"I don't normally blow-dry."

The woman stared at her, her eyes moving past her cowboy boots and jeans to the long-sleeved *Ski Winter Park* T-shirt she had tucked in, and then to her now short hair. "You don't say?" She pointed into the next room. "In there."

Reese didn't argue as she settled into the wash basin, leaning her head back into the sink, then nearly jumping up as hot, scalding water hit her head.

"Sorry, hon."

But it was over soon enough and the woman tossed a towel at

Reese who vigorously dried her hair. The woman then took the towel and wiped Reese's neck, brushing off any stray hairs.

"You sure you don't want me to blow it just a bit?"

"I'm sure." Reese ran her hand through it, the shorter strands feeling funny to her. "It'll dry soon enough."

The woman shrugged. "As you wish."

"What's your name?"

"I'm Barbara. Everyone calls me Babs."

Reese nodded and handed her a twenty and a five. "Will that cover it?"

The woman snatched the money out of her hands. "Nicely."

Back on the sidewalk, Reese walked into the sun, still rubbing her hair to dry it. She spotted Morgan coming toward her. It took a second for Morgan to even recognize her.

"It's short, I know," Reese said.

"Wow."

"I know. I told her—"

"No, I love it," Morgan said, moving closer. "It looks great on you." Their eyes met. "Sexy."

Reese felt a blush creep to her face. "Sexy, huh?"

"Definitely. In fact, I have an urge to drag you into a dark alley and have my way with you."

Reese raised her eyebrows. "Wow, that's all it takes? Get my hair cut and you want to jump my bones?"

Morgan squeezed her arm. "I don't think there's anything lacking in that area, do you?"

No. Definitely not. Not after they'd taken nearly an hour to shower this morning, still touching each other long after the hot water had run out. Reese's gaze slipped to her lips. "I want to kiss you," she said without thinking. Of course it wasn't possible, standing where they were in downtown Gunnison.

Morgan smiled and linked arms with her, leading her back to the truck. "You can steal a kiss in the truck."

And Reese did, leaning over quickly as Morgan drove them to the grocery store.

"That was hardly a kiss," Morgan complained.

"I know how my kisses distract you," she said with a grin. "Didn't want you to have an accident."

Morgan laughed and glanced at her. "I love your hair. I don't know how I'll be able to keep my hands off you."

"I don't really see that as a problem."

"No?"

Morgan reached across the seat, her fingers moving over Reese's thigh and between her legs, causing Reese to pitch forward. She closed her eyes. "Don't do this to me," she whispered.

"God, I could make love to you right now."

Reese squeezed her legs together, pressing Morgan's fingers against her. She heard Morgan's ragged breathing which matched her own. "We can't do this," she said even as her hips began rocking against Morgan's hand. "You're driving, for God's sake."

"I want you."

Reese leaned her head back, her legs opening, allowing Morgan room to touch her. And as they drove slowly through town, Morgan's hand found its way inside Reese's jeans, moving through her wetness to find her clit, hard and throbbing, aching for her touch. She stroked her fast and Reese struggled to keep her eyes opened, praying they wouldn't have an accident. How in the world could they ever explain this? But that fear soon faded as Morgan brought her closer and closer to the edge, one hand on the steering wheel, the other shoved between her legs.

Her breathing was labored and she gripped the door hard, feeling herself slipping, losing control as Morgan's fingers moved with lightning quickness against her. She bit down hard on her lip when she wanted to scream out, and she pressed Morgan's fingers against her as she climaxed.

They were both breathing fast when Morgan stopped at the light, her hand still inside Reese's pants. Morgan grinned wickedly.

"Do you think I'm in danger of sinking into the gutter after that?"

Reese laughed as she pulled Morgan's hand out of her jeans. "That was quite enjoyable," she said. "Dangerous, but enjoyable."

"I'm sorry. I wasn't thinking. I just wanted to touch you."

"I'm not complaining." She squeezed Morgan's hand, still feeling her wetness on Morgan's fingers.

And later, she just barely resisted the urge to hold Morgan's hand as they walked through the parking lot to the grocery store. Morgan smiled and bumped her shoulder playfully.

"I forgot to tell you," Morgan said. "Last week when I was at Lou's, when I got those frozen salmon steaks, he says 'I never would have thought the chief would like salmon. And can you believe this beautiful weather? Hasn't it been nice?'"

Reese laughed. "So even old Lou knows, huh?"

"The whole town knows. I swear, there's no privacy."

"Could be worse. We could be ostracized or something. At least everyone seems accepting of it."

"You know, for a small frontier town," Morgan said, "they can be awfully progressive. But being isolated like we are, there is more a sense of community. Love your neighbor and all that. There's a great sense of live and let live."

"They're also a great mix of people, I've found. There are still the old-timers and lifelong residents, but there's quite a mix of artists there too. I had no idea all those shops were actually functioning until May rolled around and they started opening up," she said as she pulled a shopping cart from the rack and pushed it through the doors.

"Most close up and head to warmer climates during the winter. I guess I just assumed you knew that, being the sheriff and all," Morgan teased.

"Well, you know, I made it a point *not* to know those things."

"Yes, I know you did. But—"

"Morgan? Is that you?"

Reese turned at the sound of the unfamiliar voice, hearing Morgan's whispered *Oh, my God* behind her.

"It *is* you," the woman gushed. "I haven't seen you in months."

Morgan gave her a quick smile. "Really. And how is Courtney or Brittany? Which was it again?"

"Amber."

"That's right. Amber. How is she?"

"She graduated and moved on. You know how that goes."

"Yes, college students tend to do that, don't they?"

Reese was surprised at the tone of Morgan's voice, and curiosity got the best of her. She stuck her hand out. "Reese Daniels, acting sheriff in Hinsdale County," she said.

"I'm Stephanie Haynes, an old friend of Morgan's. Nice to meet you." She turned to Morgan. "Wow, a sheriff? Nice to have those as friends, isn't it?"

"It has its advantages," Morgan said with a quick glance Reese's way. "We should get going."

"Wait," Stephanie said, stopping her with a touch on the arm. "Can I call you sometime? Maybe for dinner?"

Before Morgan could answer, Reese stepped forward. "Sure, maybe you can come out to the house. We could grill steaks or something." She felt Morgan move closer to her and Reese hoped she wasn't out of line. She sensed Morgan's discomfort, but she wasn't certain that was the only reason she implied they lived together. Part of her felt a need to stake her claim to Morgan.

"I see. Of course," Stephanie said. "Perhaps I'll give you a call then."

She hurried away and Morgan turned to her, smiling into her eyes. "Thank you."

Reese bowed gallantly, then walked on beside Morgan, pushing the cart. She finally laughed. "Marietta *Zula* Morgan, I can't believe I just ran into one of your exes."

CHAPTER THIRTY-SIX

"When you said tourist season would be busy, I had no idea," Reese said. "I miss you."

Morgan closed her eyes, nodding. "I miss you too. I should be home in an hour. I just have to check the campgrounds up past Slumgullion." She paused. "Did you have dinner?"

"Not yet. I'm still at the office."

Morgan smiled. "You were waiting on me. How sweet."

"You want me to pick up something at Sloan's for us?"

"You know what? I'd love a beer. You want to just meet there? Or is that too late for you?"

"I won't starve to death, if that's what you mean. I'll meet you there."

"Okay. I'll hurry."

"Be careful."

Morgan sighed as she slipped the phone back into its holster on her hip. Memorial Day Weekend was the traditional start of tourist season and this year was no exception. It seemed like every available campsite was filled. But the weather had been fabulous for the last two weeks so she wasn't really surprised at the number of people who had descended upon them. Busy couldn't adequately describe how her week had been. She and Tina had scrambled to get the water pumps going in the established campgrounds and helped Charlie's maintenance crew clear limbs from the sites where the campground hosts would live during the summer. Unfortunately, they only had four campgrounds where camp hosts lived. The other eight, Morgan and Tina would patrol, collect fees and keep clean. Well, Tina had the chore of keeping the pit toilets clean. That was one advantage to her position, Morgan thought.

But all that had left little time for Reese. And she missed her. She'd gotten home well after dark every night last week and had spent both Saturday and Sunday out. And now today, Memorial Day, things would start winding down as the locals made their trips back home to Gunnison or Pagosa Springs, or east as far as Alamosa. But Memorial Day signaled the beginning of the out-of-state visitors, so not only would the weekends be busy, but each weekday as well.

Which left little time for them. Not that they weren't together every night, no. But she was often too tired to even contemplate making love, much less doing it. So far, Reese had understood, seemingly content to hold her during the night. And each morning, when Morgan knew she needed to get out of the bed, Reese needed only to touch her, to kiss her, to make her forget all about her obligations. More often than not, they'd spent the last few minutes of each morning making love, touching until the very last moment when Morgan *had* to get up and rush through a shower.

"I'm in love with her."

The words came so easily, she wasn't surprised by them. She gripped the steering wheel tight as the meaning sunk in. Yes, she was in love with Reese. She'd been a fool to think she could remain indifferent to her, a fool to think she could stop herself

194

from falling in love. Truth was, they were so compatible in every aspect of their life, how could she *not* fall in love?

And how could Reese not fall in love too?

Morgan wasn't naïve enough to assume Reese felt the same way she did, but obviously there was *some* attachment. She knew that from the way Reese looked at her, from the way Reese made love to her. But they hadn't talked about it. They hadn't talked about anything. And in a few short months, November would be here.

And she'll leave me.

The pain gripped her heart so quickly she touched her chest, pressing her hand tight against it.

"Oh, that's good," Reese said after taking a long drink from the cold beer. "Thanks, Tracy."

"Sure." Tracy motioned to the door. "And here she is now." She smiled and picked up a fresh mug. "Hey, Morgan."

Reese turned, smiling as Morgan came over. She sat down next to her, leaning closer and briefly squeezing her arm in greeting.

"Long day, huh?"

"Yes. I can't wait to get a shower. With you," she added quietly. "Hi, Tracy. How's it going?"

Tracy slid the mug of beer in front of Morgan. "Busy. But that's good. It keeps Sloan happy. I hear the campgrounds are all full."

"Pretty much, yeah. Poor Tina. She's on garbage detail this week. She's been fighting the bears up near Cinnamon."

"Yeah. Doug Free was telling me his wife ran two of them out of their garage the other morning. He'd left it up when he went to work."

"Are they always this common?" Reese asked.

"This time of year, yes," Morgan said. "Campers bring food and trash, two things bears love. It'll settle down in late summer, then pick back up in the fall as they try to gorge before winter."

"Yell at me when you want another," Tracy said. "I've got to help Jeff with the tables." She paused. "You guys going to want dinner?"

Morgan shook her head. "Not right now. I just want to sit and relax."

When she left, Reese leaned closer. "You okay?"

Morgan met her eyes. "No."

"What's wrong?"

"I want to make love to you."

Reese recognized the look in Morgan's eyes. She loved it. "Right now?"

"I want to start in the shower and finish in our bed."

Our bed. Another thing Reese loved. She leaned closer. "I want to kiss you."

Morgan smiled. "You *always* want to kiss me."

"Is that a bad thing?"

"Remember my *no kissing* rule?"

Reese laughed and picked up her mug again. "Thank God you broke that one."

"And then my *discreet* rule?"

"It's not my fault that everyone knows."

Morgan turned on the barstool and faced her, her knees pressing against Reese's thighs. Reese turned her head, finding Morgan's smoky gaze on her.

"I want to make love to you," she said again.

It wasn't said teasingly this time. No, this time there was huskiness in Morgan's voice and desire in her eyes. Reese nodded. "Let's go home."

Morgan wasn't certain what had come over her, but she wanted Reese in the worst way. She looked in the mirror, seeing Reese's headlights behind her. Okay, so maybe she did know what had come over her. Admitting she was in love with the woman might have something to do with it. She only prayed she wouldn't let the words slip out.

She barely came to a stop before she hopped out of the truck and hurried to the front door. She had pulled her shirt off and unhooked her bra by the time Reese walked inside. She didn't say anything. She didn't want to talk.

She pressed Reese against the door, her mouth finding Reese's, moaning as their tongues met. Her fingers fumbled with the buttons on Reese's jeans as Reese cupped her breasts, her thumbs raking across her nipples. Morgan was gasping for breath when her hand snaked inside Reese's pants, shoving them down just enough to give her room.

"I want you so much," she whispered against Reese's mouth.

Reese pulled her closer, her mouth going to Morgan's neck, suckling hard, her breathing as labored as Morgan's.

Morgan spread her fingers, cupping Reese, feeling her wetness soak her hand. She moaned as her fingers moved through her silkiness, closing her eyes as her fingers filled Reese. Reese's teeth nipped at her neck as her hips rocked against Morgan's hand, her panting causing Morgan to move faster, pumping hard into her, loving the tightening of Reese's muscles against her fingers.

"Come for me," she breathed into Reese's ear. "Come for me."

She didn't have to wait long. She felt the familiar trembling as Reese neared orgasm, she recognized the sounds Reese made when she was about to climax. And seconds later, with one last thrust, Reese called out, muffling her scream against Morgan's neck, before nearly collapsing in her arms.

Morgan pulled her fingers out but didn't move, standing there pressed against Reese, feeling Reese's heart beating against her breasts, listening to the quick intake of air as Reese tried to catch her breath. She closed her eyes.

I love you.

Three little words that shouldn't cause this much pain. But they did. She finally stirred, her lips moving slowly across Reese's face, finding her lips, kissing them gently. When she pulled back and looked into Reese's eyes, she swore she could see her love reflected back at her. But Reese lowered her gaze, kissing her mouth once again, so tenderly Morgan nearly cried.

"Shower? Then bed?" Reese smiled against her mouth. "Wasn't that the order?"

"So I started early," Morgan said. "I'll have that shower with you now, though."

CHAPTER THIRTY-SEVEN

Morgan knew it was time to get up, but she just couldn't bring herself to pull out of Reese's arms. It had been two weeks since she'd admitted she was in love with her. Two weeks since the night of her sexual frenzy. Reese must have thought she was insatiable, and she'd felt that way. She couldn't stop touching her. She couldn't stop *wanting* her. It was the early morning hours before they finally fell into an exhausted sleep.

And again, like when the no kissing rule was broken, there was a slight shift in their relationship. It was obvious to her, if not Reese. Their touches were more tender, if that were even possible. Their kisses seemed to hold more meaning. The looks that passed between them were unguarded, hinting at the underlying passion that always simmered just below the surface, hinting at love. Or maybe she just saw that because that's what she wanted to see. Maybe all of this was simply her imagination because she'd accepted the fact that she was in love with Reese.

And she'd also accepted the fact that Reese would be leaving. Nothing had changed in that respect. They didn't talk about it. Just like they never talked about the possibility of Reese staying. It was not a subject that either of them broached.

But as mid-June threatened to turn into late June, the months and weeks moved by faster and faster, and November loomed, no longer a month just lurking in the distance. It was a month that was creeping up on them, a month that would shatter her world.

She closed her eyes tightly, her heart aching. She kept it all in—the worry, the fear—putting on a happy face, pretending this arrangement was just fine, just what she expected. Truth was, she felt like she would explode if she didn't get it out. But not to Reese. Never to Reese. She moved her lips, letting them linger on Reese's skin, smiling as Reese stirred.

She finally pulled away, quietly so as to not wake Reese. She dressed quickly, deciding to put in an appearance at her own house and shower there. She hadn't actually set foot in her house since May. And after her shower, she would find Tina, take her someplace where they could have some privacy...and talk.

CHAPTER THIRTY-EIGHT

"You're being awful secretive about this," Tina said as Morgan drove them down a quiet forest road.

"Because I want to talk and I don't want to be interrupted."

"Yeah? So what's our subject?"

Morgan rolled her eyes. "You know very well what the subject is."

"Okay. Then why the need for privacy? Everyone already *knows* you two are together."

Morgan sighed. "That's just it. We're not really *together*."

"Honey, I've seen the two of you. You can barely keep your hands off each other, much less your eyes. Do you think people can't see the way you look at each other?"

"I'm not talking about that." She pulled to a stop in a small grove of aspens, their tiny leaves fluttering on the trees, giving truth to their name, the *quaking* aspen. She closed her door quietly, not wanting to disturb the stillness. She leaned on the bed of the truck, looking at Tina across the way. "I'm in love with her."

Tina snorted. "You brought me all the way out here to tell me that? Like I don't already know."

"You don't understand. I can't be in love with her." She walked around to the back of the truck and lowered the tailgate. She sat down heavily and let out a deep sigh. "We had rules, you know."

"What are you talking about?" Tina asked as she joined her on the tailgate.

"Our arrangement. The agreement was a physical, sexual affair. Nothing more." Morgan smiled. "I even had a no kissing rule at first. And a *let's be discreet* rule."

"Well, I know you broke one of them. I'll assume you broke the kissing rule too."

"I'd thought, if it was just a physical affair, the best way to keep it at that level was no kissing. Kissing is very intimate."

"But that didn't last?"

Morgan shook her head. "A month."

"Wow. That long?"

Morgan lowered her head. "She's leaving in November, Tina."

"You don't know that for sure. Has she said so?"

"She hasn't said she's *not* leaving. She made it perfectly clear to everyone that she was only staying the one year. She made that perfectly clear to me."

"But that was before you two—"

"No. That was part of the agreement. She was only going to be here until November. Our *affair* would last that long."

"But it's no longer an affair," Tina said. "Right?"

"It ceased being an affair months ago. For Reese too. I know she doesn't look at it that way. Hell, we're practically living together."

"What do you mean *practically*?"

"I know. And I told myself I wasn't going to fall in love with her. I told myself I could keep it strictly physical." She turned and looked at Tina. "But when I'm with her, damn, we're so compatible. In *everything*. Not just sex. Everything. We like the same food, the same wine. We both like to hike and get out in the woods. We never argue or bicker about anything. It's so *easy* to be with her. And, my God, the sex. Never in my life did I think I'd have such an active sex life. Never."

"Don't rub it in. Twenty years and a couple of kids tend to put a damper on things."

"Sorry."

"So why don't you just tell her?"

"No, I'm not going to tell her. That would just be stupid. I don't want her to feel guilty when she leaves here. I'm the one who broke the damn rule, not her."

"But, Morgan, how do you know not her? I mean, I've seen the two of you together. I've seen the way she looks at you. How do you know she's not in love with you too?"

"Don't you think she would have said something?"

Tina laughed. "Oh, yeah. Right. Like you have."

"It's different. She's the one planning to leave. Not me."

"Then why don't you just talk about it?"

"Because I don't want to embarrass myself."

"Telling someone you love them shouldn't be an embarrassment."

"Of course it's an embarrassment if it's one-sided. *Guess what, Reese? I broke another rule.*" Morgan shrugged. "No. I'm not going to tell her."

"I think that's a mistake. I think you're both being stubborn about these stupid rules you started out with and neither wants to be the one to admit they crossed the line." Tina bumped her arm. "Stubborn and *immature*."

"Immature? Immature would be not being able to keep the relationship where it was meant to be. Immature would be to fall in love. But keeping the secret inside? That's not being immature," Morgan said as she tapped her chest. "That's being an adult."

Tina shook her head. "No, that's being just plain stupid."

CHAPTER THIRTY-NINE

Reese stood in front of Eloise's desk, turning a circle, a frown on her face as she looked around. She tapped Eloise's desk. "We don't have a jail." She held up her hands. "Why don't we have a jail, Eloise?"

"What do we need a jail for?"

"Oh, I don't know. We're the sheriff's office. Surely sometime in the last *century* we've needed a jail," she said sarcastically.

Eloise stared blankly at her. "You've been here eight months. You're just now discovering we don't have a jail?"

Reese shrugged. "So if I need one, what do we do? Lock them in the supply closet?"

Eloise flicked her eyes as if bored with the conversation. Reese arched an eyebrow, waiting. Eloise sighed.

"There are two cells in the museum. Well, only one of them locks though."

"In the museum? Our jail cells are in the museum?" Reese paused. "I didn't even know we had a museum."

Eloise stared at her blankly. "They're open Memorial Day through Labor Day. The building used to be the old jail from back in the day. They left the cells up when they turned it into a museum."

"I see. And have we ever used them?"

"Not that I'm aware of."

Amazing, Reese thought. The jail cells were in a museum. A museum she didn't even know existed. She shook her head, then moved to her own office, pausing again. "Where's Googan?"

"I have no idea."

"Well, why don't you call him on the radio? Rouse him up."

"Don't you think he gets tired of you checking up on him ten, fifteen times a day?"

"I just want to make sure he's okay."

"His doctor released him."

"Doesn't hurt to check." She motioned to the radio. "Call him, would you?"

"I swear," Eloise mumbled under her breath as she picked up the radio. "Googan? Come in. The Chief's looking for you." She waited. "What's your...your ten-thirty?"

"It's ten-twenty," Reese said. "How many times have I told you? Ten-twenty."

"Where are you?" Eloise said instead, daring Reese to correct her.

Reese paced behind her chair. "Call him again," she said. She hated when he didn't answer. He'd been back three weeks, and yes, she checked on him constantly.

"Googan? Come in," Eloise said again.

"Maybe something happened. Maybe I should go out and look for him," Reese said quickly.

They both looked up as the bell jingled over the door. Googan stood there, watching them.

Reese smiled. "See? I told you he was okay." She turned quickly and went into her office, embarrassed. Really, she needed to let it go. Googan was fine. His limp was barely discernable. She had to stop worrying that he was going to drive off into one of the canyons again. A freak accident, that's all.

So she sat down and tapped the mouse, scattering the screen saver. There were no reports to fill out, no budgets to go over. No crime, no nothing. So she did what she usually did in the afternoons. She played solitaire on the computer.

She was into her second game when Eloise yelled that she had a call.

"What line?"

"The only one that's blinking," Eloise barked from the other room.

"Can we at least pretend to have some sort of professionalism here? We do have an intercom, you know," she yelled back. She picked up the phone. "Reese Daniels. How can I help you?"

"Chief Daniels, good to hear your voice again."

Reese frowned. The man's voice was familiar, but she couldn't place it.

"It's Michael Stewart," he said.

Reese smiled. "I knew I recognized your voice. How the hell are you?"

"We're doing great. The ski season ended late after that big storm in April. And summer's in full swing. How about you? They keeping you busy there?"

She laughed. "No, can't say they are. It's very tame here compared to Winter Park."

"No doubt. Actually, that's really the reason I'm calling. We want you to come back."

The smile left her face and she stared at the phone. *Come back?* "What about Richard?"

"Oh, they got a divorce. He moved to Denver and is with some law firm now." He paused. "Cheri is still here though."

"I see. And what about your current police chief?"

"Interim only. He knew that coming in. But he's a little young for the job. Needs more seasoning. He hasn't quite learned how to pamper the tourists yet. We like your experience, Reese."

She leaned back in her chair. Wow. Just like that, she had her old job back. If she wanted it. "Well, I appreciate the offer,

Michael. You know I'm locked in here until November."

"Surely you can get out of that?"

"I'll have to see. I'd hate to put them in a bind," she said.

"Okay. Do what you can. We're anxious to get you back."

"Sure. I'll get back with you, Michael."

Yeah. Just like that. She spun her chair around, looking out the small back window to the street behind the sheriff's office. She could see Doris Newman walking to her tiny wood frame house, a sack of groceries in her arms that she'd just gotten at Lou's. And she knew if she kept watching, her husband Larry would get home from his job at Thompson's Ranch at about a quarter to five. And sometimes, as a treat, Larry and Doris would walk over to Sloan's for dinner instead of Doris cooking. She knew all that just from watching them these last few months. She didn't know they had a goddamn museum in town, but she knew Doris and Larry's daily routine.

She spun back around to her desk, wondering when it happened, this connection she had with the town and its people. No involvements, remember? One year of exile then back to the real world. These people got along fine before she got here and they'd be just fine when she left.

She rubbed her eyes. Leaving Morgan would be the hardest, of course. She'd been dreading it actually. They never discussed it, but it was always there. November was tapping on the door. Michael Stewart didn't want to wait until November. He wanted her now. But even though she knew they could place Googan back in charge, she just wasn't prepared to leave now. She wasn't *emotionally* prepared to leave, as scary as that was. Truth was, she wasn't prepared to leave Morgan.

Well, she needed to talk to her. She needed to tell her. Maybe she could feel her out and see how she took the news. If Morgan acted upset or disappointed, then maybe Reese could entertain the idea of staying in Lake City another year.

What am I thinking?

It's Winter Park. Her dream job. She'd have to be crazy to turn it down.

207

CHAPTER FORTY

Reese found Morgan on the back deck of the cabin, sipping a glass of wine. She smiled as she saw the two steaks already seasoned, just waiting for the charcoal to heat.

"What's the occasion?" she asked as she bent down and kissed Morgan on the lips.

"It's just so beautiful out," Morgan said. "And we don't take advantage of the picnic table nearly enough." She caught Reese's hand as she walked past and squeezed. "Did you have a good day?"

Reese laughed. "Yeah, but it'd be good to have a crime spree or something every once in a while." She picked up the bottle of wine and filled the glass Morgan had placed there for her. She topped off Morgan's as well. She realized her hand was shaking as she put the bottle back down. She was nervous. Far more nervous than she should be.

She sat beside Morgan, pulling the deck chair closer. And as natural as can be, they found their hands touching, their fingers entwined. God, she was going to miss this. But there was no sense putting if off. She took a deep breath, trying to calm her nerves.

"Got a call today," she said as nonchalantly as possible. "From Winter Park." She felt Morgan's fingers tighten slightly against her own.

"Oh, yeah?"

"Seems the mayor and his wife got a divorce. He moved to Denver, and, well, they want me to come back."

She stared at Morgan, trying to judge her reaction. The cheerful smile Morgan flashed couldn't hide the misgiving in her eyes.

"How wonderful! I know you liked it there."

Reese nodded. "Yeah, I did. And I know the people there."

"Well, I think that's great." She squeezed Reese's hand. "And you know, maybe you and the mayor's wife can try it again," she teased.

Reese didn't say anything as Morgan got up. She pointed to the steaks.

"Do you mind putting those on? I want to grab a quick shower."

Reese nodded. "Sure."

She didn't know what to make of Morgan's reaction. Her cheerfulness was forced, she could tell that. But she'd thought perhaps Morgan might ask her to stay. Oh, well. Maybe she'd read too much into their relationship. Maybe Morgan wasn't going to be all that upset when she left after all.

Maybe she wouldn't even miss her.

Morgan barely made it into the bathroom before her heart broke completely. She leaned on the counter, taking deep breaths. It wasn't supposed to hurt this much. It wasn't like it was unexpected. But it was July. Three more months to live with the knowledge that Reese was going back to Winter Park.

She met her eyes in the mirror, letting her tears fall without even trying to stop them. Broken hearts deserved tears, at least. But when the tears turned to sobs, she quickly shed her clothes and stepped into the shower, letting the warm water wash her tears away. She had no idea how she was going to make it through dinner. She could barely make it through a shower.

She sobbed again, leaning against the wall and wrapping her arms around herself, praying the pain would go away.

It didn't.

Going through the motions of dinner was the hardest thing she'd ever had to do. Trying to appear as though everything were perfectly normal, perfectly fine. Trying to make conversation without crying. She couldn't look at Reese. She knew if she looked into her eyes she would break down. She knew she would make a complete fool of herself and beg her to stay. So she put on a brave face, smiling to the extreme she knew, but it was the only way to keep from crying. Reese didn't comment on her behavior. In fact, Reese seemed far too quiet. Perhaps it was because Morgan was chatting away, pulling subjects out of the air, anything to avoid a lull in the conversation where they might have to actually talk about something that mattered.

Like Reese leaving.

And later, after they'd both pushed the food around on their plates, after she'd cleaned up dinner while Reese showered, she crawled into bed beside Reese, moving into her arms, relishing what she knew would be their last night together. She just couldn't go on pretending any longer. No, she would end this *affair*. She didn't think she could survive if she didn't.

Even now, as Reese rolled them over, as she settled her weight between her thighs, Morgan felt her heart breaking a little more, felt tears sting her eyes. She pulled Reese close, letting her lips move across her skin, memorizing her taste, her smell. She squeezed her eyes shut.

I love you.

But there were no words spoken as they made love to each other. Reese's hands were strong, familiar, as they moved across her body, touching her in all the secret places that only Reese knew. Morgan felt a tear slide down her face as Reese suckled her breast, gently and tenderly loving her. Morgan arched into her, opening her legs, inviting Reese inside.

As Reese's fingers filled her, they moved together slowly, effortlessly. Morgan pulled Reese's mouth from her breast, bringing her to her lips, her tongue sliding over Reese's before sucking it inside her mouth. She heard Reese moan, felt her hips buck against her own, forcing Reese's fingers deeper inside her.

She wanted to make it last, she wanted to feel Reese within her forever, but much too soon her orgasm threatened, her hips moving faster and faster as Reese rhythmically thrust inside her. But Reese suddenly stopped, pulling her fingers away as she moved down Morgan's body.

"*Yes*," she breathed. "With your mouth."

This, too, she didn't have time to savor. Reese cupped her hips, bringing Morgan to her waiting mouth. But Morgan was so ready, so close, that only the briefest of touches from Reese's tongue pushed her over the edge. She squeezed her legs tight, holding Reese to her, crying out as Reese sucked her clit into her mouth.

"Oh, *God*, Reese," she cried, her head falling back against the pillow as Reese continued to suckle her. She closed her eyes tight, giving in to the feel of Reese's mouth on her, her tongue moving inside her. She came again, her hips lifting off the bed, pressing against Reese's mouth as Reese drained the last breath from her.

"Reese—" she whispered, her voice thick with unshed tears.

I love you.

Morgan stirred as the ringing of the phone woke her. Reese pulled away, blindly reaching out for it. Morgan's eyes slipped shut again as she listened to Reese's voice. There was no urgency, so she wasn't worried about the early morning phone call. She was too tired. Their lovemaking had taken them well past midnight.

"I've got to go," Reese said as she bent down and kissed Morgan, her lips lingering.

"What's wrong?" she asked sleepily.

"Thompson's got some cattle out. They want me to block off the road, that's all." Reese kissed her again. "Go back to sleep."

"Uh-huh," she murmured as she rolled over, snuggling against Reese's pillow. She never heard Reese leave as she drifted off to sleep, but she woke only a short time later, feeling the emptiness of the bed.

And the emptiness of her heart.

She tossed off the covers and got up, rubbing her tired eyes as she shuffled into the bathroom. It would do no good to linger here. She would take a quick shower and pack her things...and go home. Except that it felt like she was leaving home. She doubted her little Forest Service house would ever feel like home again.

She tried not to think as she moved from room to room, picking up her things. The red robe that hung behind the door in the bathroom. Her toothbrush. Jeans and shirts. A few paperback books. The framed picture of her and Jackson that she'd brought over. In the kitchen, she spotted the corkscrew she'd bought so that they wouldn't have to use Reese's Swiss Army knife anymore. She smiled as she held it, the smile soon disappearing as tears took its place. She put the corkscrew back, leaving it for Reese.

She took one last look around, her eyes swimming in tears. There was no need to leave a note.

CHAPTER FORTY-ONE

Reese pulled to a stop beside her cabin, hoping Morgan's truck would be there. She hadn't been able to reach her all day. Each time she called, it went to voice mail. She finally got hold of Charlie.

"Oh, she's out and about. You know cell service is iffy up in the mountains."

So she'd left it at that, even though she had an uneasy feeling all day. The only thing normal about last night was when they made love. But dinner was strained, conversation forced. And oddly, no mention of her leaving. She'd have thought they would have at least discussed it. Something. But no. Morgan acted as if Reese had never mentioned Winter Park.

She went inside and closed the door and it struck her immediately. It was empty. She tilted her head, listening to the quiet. She made herself move, going into their bedroom, seeing the empty space where Jackson's picture used to sit. She swallowed hard, then moved to the bathroom, looking at the empty hook behind the door where Morgan's robe usually hung.

"So, just like that," she said.

She couldn't believe the heaviness of her heart, couldn't believe how much it hurt to know Morgan had left. To know Morgan wasn't coming back.

CHAPTER FORTY-TWO

"This is insane."

"Stop it."

"I'm just saying—"

"I know what you're saying, Tina. But it doesn't matter. This is best."

"If you don't talk to her, I will."

Morgan whipped her head around. "Don't you dare."

"So it's going to be like this for the next three months? You not answering your phone? You staying out in the woods until dark? Me and Berta and Charlie having to lie for you?"

"She's not stupid, Tina. She knows why I left. And she'll leave it alone. And then we can pretend that nothing was ever between us, and should we meet here at Sloan's, we'll be civil to each other and when November gets here, she'll leave for good. And hopefully by then, I'll be over her." Morgan knew she'd never be over Reese, but she wasn't going to tell Tina this. She'd avoided

Reese for two days. She figured that was all Reese would give her. Tonight, Reese would find her. And she didn't want it to be alone. So she'd made Tina come with her to Sloan's. She would speak privately with Reese, sure. But she didn't want to be alone.

"You two haven't been in here together in a long time," Tracy said. "Where's Reese?"

Morgan glanced at Tina. "We're kinda, well, we kinda cooled things off," Morgan said.

Tina shook her head. "Reese got an offer from Winter Park to get her old job back. She's leaving, so Morgan bailed."

"Tina, please," Morgan whispered.

"It's just Tracy. Like I'm not going to fill her in later anyway."

"So she's really leaving? I thought you two were so good together. I mean, you seemed so happy," Tracy said.

"Happy? Yes. We always knew it was temporary though. She was planning on leaving in November whether Winter Park called or not," Morgan said. "I just thought it was better to end things now. No sense—" But her voice trailed away as Reese walked in the door, their eyes meeting across the room. Morgan's heart skipped a beat and she had a difficult time catching her breath.

"Hi, ladies," Reese said as she walked over.

"Get you a beer, Chief?"

"Sure, Tracy. Thanks."

Reese stood beside Morgan, but Morgan purposefully kept her gaze away. Reese finally touched her shoulder. "Can we talk?"

Morgan wanted to say *no*, but she knew she at least owed Reese an explanation. Tina moved to get up, but Morgan stopped her. "We'll go to a booth," she said.

She kept her hands folded together on the table, unable to look at Reese. If she looked at her, all her brave words would mean nothing. She'd spent most of the day trying to harden her heart, knowing that was the only way to get through this.

"What's up, Morgan?" Reese asked quietly.

"What do you mean?"

"Come on, you know what I mean."

Morgan cleared her throat, still not meeting Reese's eyes. "You'll be leaving soon. I'm sure you have a lot of things to take care of. Packing to do."

"No. I don't have that much to pack."

Morgan finally looked at her, trying so hard to keep her gaze steady. "Well, honestly, I just didn't see the point of going on like we were. I mean, I had a good time and all, but it's time to put an end to it." She shrugged. "It's over. We had our fun."

"Just like that? I don't get a say in it?"

Morgan tried to smile. "You laid the ground rules, Reese. And I think you said if one of us no longer enjoyed it, we could stop."

Reese stared at her. "So you're stopping because you didn't enjoy it any longer?" She leaned closer. "Is that why you screamed my name when we made love that last night? Because you no longer enjoyed it?"

"Sex is sex, Reese," she said cruelly. "We can find it anywhere. Like you with the mayor's wife or me with a cute tourist. It's time to move on." She tried to ignore the pain she saw in Reese's eyes. Her words hurt, she knew. And they were uncalled for. But she didn't want to be the only one hurting.

Reese stood up. "Well, you just made leaving a hell of a lot easier. Thanks."

Morgan watched her go, surprised she was able to stop herself from running after her. She shook her head when Tina would have come over. She didn't want to talk. She got up slowly, not looking at anyone as she walked out the door.

Once home, she locked the door and stripped off her clothes and crawled into bed.

And she cried.

She cried for all that was lost and all that could have been. She cried because she was alone and she missed Jackson. She cried because her heart ached like it had never ached before. She cried because she was in love. And she cried because she'd intentionally hurt the one person she cared most about in the world. The person she wanted to spend the rest of her life with. The person who was walking out of her world.

So she cried.

CHAPTER FORTY-THREE

"I'm sorry, Ron, but it's only a few months. Googan can handle things."

"We don't want Googan to handle things, Chief. You agreed to stay until November."

"They offered me the job now. I can't turn it down," she said.

"Look, I understand Lake City is not Winter Park. I understand the limitations we have here. But a contract is a contract. They have their own interim police chief. A few more months won't hurt them either."

Reese knew Brightmen would never go for her leaving early, but she at least wanted to try. She had to get away. She couldn't sleep at night. She couldn't stand the emptiness of the cabin. And each time she saw Morgan in town, she felt a tightness in her chest she didn't understand.

Oh, hell, who was she kidding? She understood it perfectly.

It was called love, something she didn't have a whole lot of experience with. She shouldn't be surprised she'd fallen in love with Morgan. All those months of playing house, of making love, of *being* together, how could she not? The months she'd spent with Morgan were the happiest of her life. And they had come to a screeching halt.

Because Morgan had no trouble leaving her. Morgan had no trouble ending things. Morgan was going on about her life. She wasn't pining for her. She wasn't suffering though sleepless nights because Reese wasn't in her bed. She wasn't dreading going home to an empty house. No. She ended things as easily as she'd started them with no remorse or heartache.

Why she ended things early, Reese still couldn't understand. It was too good between them, despite Morgan's words that *sex was sex*. When they were together, it was just so *right*. Did Morgan suspect that Reese had fallen in love? Did Morgan run because of that?

CHAPTER FORTY-FOUR

"I swear I've never seen you like this."

Morgan looked up from the monthly budget report she was reviewing and offered Charlie a weak smile. "Sorry. I'll be fine."

"Come into my office, Morgan."

Morgan took a deep breath and let it out slowly. Charlie was playing the father figure, she knew. But she just wasn't in the mood to talk about it.

"Close the door," he said as she followed him in. "Now, you want to tell me what's going on? I've heard bits and pieces from Tina and Berta, but I'd rather hear it from you."

She shrugged. "Reese is leaving. We ended things. That's it."

"Yeah, I heard Winter Park offered her a job. Ron Brightmen said Reese had called asking out of her contract so she could leave now."

Morgan's eyes widened. Wow. Reese couldn't wait to get out of here, could she? Oh, well. The sooner the better. She'd just as soon not have to spend the next three months avoiding her at Sloan's.

"Anyway, I got something I want to talk to you about." He leaned back in his chair and smiled. "You know, I'm out of here at the end of August."

"You don't have to remind me, Charlie. The calendar with the big Xs on it does just fine."

He laughed. "When you get close to retirement after nearly thirty years, you'll be marking off the days too."

"I'm happy for you. I really am. It's just, for us, they're going to bring in some old blowhard with rules, and I'll have to go back to wearing those god-awful uniforms again."

"Well, then that's where I think you'll be happy." He passed her a letter to read. "I recommended you for the job, Morgan. They agreed."

"*What*? Me?" She glanced at the letter, words jumping out at her—*promotion, manager, new budget, new position*. She looked up. "What the hell?"

"You deserve it. You put in your time. Plus, as I pointed out to them, you know the area, you know the people."

"Yeah, but I don't know anything about running this office, Charlie. How am I going to put together a budget each year? And those damn monthly reports you have to send in, how am I—"

"Oh, hell, Morgan, you already do the work. I just put it all together. It's mostly BS paperwork anyway. You know that."

She stood and walked across the room, still holding the letter. To say she was floored, to say she was *shocked* was an understatement. It never even occurred to her that they would promote her. She was too young, she was a female, and she only had fifteen years in the service. All strikes against her. She turned slowly and smiled at him. "Damn."

"I also got a new full-time position approved. I know we don't need it in the winter, but in the summer, you run yourself ragged. And knowing you, you're not going to sit your ass in this chair like I do. You're going to want to be out."

"When I first started here, you were out too, Charlie."

He nodded. "Until I knew I could trust you to do all the things that needed to get done."

She smiled as she went to him, bending down to give him a quick hug. "Thank you, Charlie. This means so much to me. It really does."

"Like I said, you deserve it."

"Thanks. You've brightened up my rather miserable week."

But that night, as she sat at home alone—staring at the muted TV—she couldn't muster up the enthusiasm she'd had earlier in the day. It was news she wanted to share with someone. Not a friend, like Tina or Tracy. But with a lover. Someone who would be proud of her accomplishment, someone who would smile and bring her into a tight hug, and someone who would tell her she loved her.

She turned the TV off and stretched out on the old sofa, folding her hands behind her head as she stared off into space, unable to stop her tears, unable to ease the awful ache in her heart.

CHAPTER FORTY-FIVE

Reese drove slowly past Sloan's Bar, thankful Morgan's truck wasn't parked out front. Hopefully, it meant she was at home. Because Reese couldn't go another day without speaking to her. If Morgan wanted to end things, fine. But Reese thought she at least was owed an explanation. She didn't believe for a moment Morgan's excuse of not enjoying it any longer.

She stood on Morgan's porch for the longest time, surprised by how nervous she was, afraid of what Morgan might say to her. She finally took a deep breath and knocked. She waited a few minutes longer, then knocked again.

"Morgan? Come on. I just want to talk to you." She heard movement, but the door didn't open.

"Just go away," Morgan said from behind the door.

"No. I want to talk to you."

"Please, Reese? Just leave."

"Why won't you talk to me?" She tilted her head, listening.

"Look, I don't want to come in. We can just stand here on the porch. I just want to talk. Please?" She leaned her head against the door. "Please?" she asked quietly.

She stepped back when the door slowly opened. Morgan's eyes were damp, her nose red. *Had she been crying?*

"I miss you," she whispered. "I miss you so much."

Morgan shook her head. "Don't. Don't do this."

"Do you miss me?" she asked.

Morgan wiped her cheek then met her eyes. "Yes. Yes, I miss you."

"Then why? Why are we doing this?"

"Because you're leaving, Reese. That's why."

"I'm not leaving until November."

Morgan's tears fell freely now, and Reese didn't know what to do. She took a step forward, but Morgan held her hand out, stopping her. "No. Don't. Just leave. I can't do this."

"Why, Morgan?" *Why are we doing this? Why are you crying?*

"Do you think I won't miss you when November comes?" Morgan tried to smile through her tears. "I thought I'd practice first. Maybe by November...well, maybe I won't miss you so much."

Reese stared into her eyes. "Tell me why you're crying."

Morgan shook her head and backed up. "Please go now, Reese. Don't come by anymore, okay?"

"Wait," Reese said quickly. She stuck her hand out, stopping the door before Morgan closed it in her face. She felt like her heart was being ripped from her chest, and she couldn't stand to see Morgan cry.

"No. Just go. Please?"

"Did you fall in love with me, Morgan? Is that why you're crying?"

The pained look on Morgan's face told her everything she needed to know. That, and the sobs that shook her as Morgan closed the door. She stood there, listening to Morgan cry, hating her own tears that were falling. She put her palm on the door, knowing Morgan was leaning against the door on the other side.

Leaning against the door and crying. Crying for her.

Because she loved her.

She turned, as if in a daze. Morgan loved her. She didn't end things because she was tired of it. She ended it because Reese had told her Winter Park had called. She ended it because Reese was leaving.

She stared into the night sky, the stars twinkling overhead, their light blurred by the dampness in her eyes.

"Morgan loves me," she said out loud. She finally smiled. "She loves me and she doesn't want me to leave."

She drove quickly to her office, unlocking the door but not bothering with the main lights. Inside her private office, she pulled out a piece of paper where she'd scribbled a phone number. She didn't hesitate as she picked up the phone and dialed.

"Michael? It's Reese Daniels." She paused. "I changed my mind."

CHAPTER FORTY-SIX

For the first time ever, Morgan called in sick. For one thing, she looked frightful. Her eyes were red and puffy, evidence of how she spent her night. And frankly, she couldn't muster the energy to pretend she was fine any longer. She was miserable. As miserable and depressed as she could ever recall being.

One look into Reese's eyes brought the depth of her love to the surface and only served to magnify her aching heart.

Did you fall in love with me, Morgan? Is that why you're crying?

"Yes," she whispered.

She wrapped her arms around herself, desperately wanting— *needing*—a hug. She knew she had to snap out of this. She knew she had to get over it. But right now, she hurt too much to do anything. So she sank back down into the corner of the sofa and tucked her legs under her, staring at the far wall, staring at nothing, fearing she was falling apart.

Reese couldn't get the silly grin off her face. And she couldn't wait to get to Morgan. She wasn't answering her cell, but that wasn't surprising. What was surprising was Tina's admission that she'd stayed home sick. Morgan was never sick.

Reese knew it was her fault. She knew Morgan's tears were because of her. And now she was about to put an end to those tears.

Last night after she'd called Michael Stewart to tell him she wasn't going back to Winter Park after all, she'd also called Ron Brightmen. He was thrilled to learn she was staying. And he was more than happy to extend the use of his cabin for as long as she needed.

And this morning, bright and early, she'd driven into Gunnison, and spent the next hour touching, holding and *cuddling* puppies at the animal shelter.

She looked over at the ball of fur beside her and scratched the little ear. "I hope your new mommy isn't mad at us." They'd told her his mother was a yellow Labrador, but the father was unknown. There were four puppies in the litter and they all looked like labs to her, but the staff picked this one out, saying he looked just like his mother. Now she only hoped his *new* mother would love him.

She parked beside Morgan's truck, then rolled the windows up some in hers so the puppy wouldn't crawl out. "Don't chew on anything important," she told him as she got out. The nervousness she felt last night was magnified tenfold today. Today she would tell Morgan she loved her. Today she would ask Morgan to share her life with her.

But this time she didn't hesitate as she knocked on the door. They'd wasted enough time.

"Morgan? It's me. Open up." She knocked again, then heard footsteps on the other side.

"Please go away."

She smiled. "Are we going to do this again? You know I'm not going away, now open the door."

"No."

"Please open the door, Zula," she said.

Finally, the door opened and Morgan stood there, her eyes swimming in tears. "You're killing me," she whispered.

"No. Never." Reese reached for her. "Come here."

"No."

"Yes," she said. She pulled Morgan into her arms, her heart breaking as Morgan's sobs shook her. "Don't cry, sweetheart."

"I'm sorry," Morgan whispered as she clung to her. "I'm dying here."

Reese closed her eyes, holding Morgan tight, feeling complete again, *whole* again with Morgan in her arms.

"I can't leave you," she said. "I fell in love with you too, Morgan." Morgan tried to pull away, but Reese held her tight. "When I told you Winter Park called, I wanted you to ask me to stay. But you didn't. You seemed almost happy."

"Oh, my God. I thought you *wanted* to go. That's why I pretended to be happy." Morgan wiped at her tears. "You love me?" she asked weakly.

"With all my heart." Reese tilted her face up, meeting her eyes. "I never thought I could have this, could feel this way about someone. I never thought I'd find someone to love me. I never thought I'd want to share my life with someone. I don't want to leave here, Morgan. I don't want to leave *you*."

"Oh, Reese," she whispered. "I love you. I've loved you for so long." Her tears fell again and she let them. "When you said you were leaving, I just wanted to die. I just wanted to curl up and die."

"I'm so sorry." She kissed her lips softly, tasting her tears. "I love you, Morgan. I want you to come back home."

"Yes." Morgan smiled as she buried her face against Reese's neck. "Yes."

A high-pitched puppy bark pulled them apart and Morgan looked at her questioningly.

"Oh, yeah," Reese said. "I kinda forgot about him."

"Him who?"

Reese took her hand and led her to the truck. "I thought, well,

I've never had a pet before. And you had Jackson and he'll always be yours." She stopped before opening the door. "I thought it'd be nice to have one together. One that would be *ours*."

Again tears, and Reese smiled. "You've got to quit crying. You're giving me a complex."

But Morgan flung herself into Reese's arms, nearly knocking her over. "God, I love you so much. A *puppy*?" Then she quickly pushed Reese out of the way as she opened the door, laughing as she scooped up the yellow ball of fur.

Reese stood back, watching as the tiny pink tongue kissed away Morgan's tears, and she felt her heart swell with emotion.

Yeah, it felt so *damn* good to be in love.

CHAPTER FORTY-SEVEN

Reese stood looking out the window to the nearly deserted street, wondering if the light dusting of snow would change their plans. Morgan wanted to hike the meadow trail to the river and let Cody get some play time in the water. It had become a once a week ritual, followed by burgers and beer at Sloan's.

She was still amazed at how much her life had changed, and how much she *loved* all the changes. After Charlie retired, they bought his cabin along with the two horses he was going to ship off to Thompson's Ranch. The house was bigger than they needed, bigger than either of them had lived in before, but it was slowly becoming their place and no longer Charlie's.

The late summer had been idyllic as they grew comfortable in their love and they'd slipped back into their familiar routine of spending most of their time alone, cooking, talking, hiking...and loving.

And now winter was upon them again and they'd come full

circle. And added one furry member to their family. She felt like the luckiest person alive.

"I guess I'm going to head out," Eloise said.

Reese nodded. "Where's Googan?"

"If I had to guess, he's called it a day and is over at Sloan's." Eloise motioned out the window. "She's here."

Reese turned, smiling broadly as Morgan got out of her truck, Cody right behind her. "That's a pretty sight now, isn't it?"

Eloise just smiled and shook her head as Morgan and Cody burst through the door.

"Hi, Eloise," Morgan said. "On your way out?"

"Yes. How are the roads?"

"Oh, they're fine. Slushy."

"Well, you two have a good evening. See you tomorrow, Chief."

"Drive carefully."

The door had barely closed before they moved together, Morgan pulling her close for a kiss.

"I missed you today," she said.

Reese smiled. "Is that right?" Reese cupped her hips and brought Morgan flush against her, loving the tiny moan Morgan uttered.

"Don't start," Morgan whispered against her mouth. "You promised me a hike."

"It's cold out," Reese said, her hands sliding up to Morgan's breasts.

"What about Cody?"

"He'll understand." Reese's finger circled Morgan's nipple, eliciting another moan.

"Someone could come in."

"I'll lock the door," she murmured between kisses.

Morgan laughed. "You're insatiable."

"I'm just in love, *Zula*."

Morgan pulled back, meeting her eyes. "I love you too, *Clarice*," she said softly as she pulled Reese again to her mouth.

And so their hike was forgotten, and Cody too, as he settled himself on the rug, waiting for their passion to be sated. Reese had a feeling he would be waiting longer today than usual as Morgan's hands fumbled with her jeans.

Insatiable and in love.

Yes, a wonderful state to be in.

Publications from
Bella Books, Inc.
The best in contemporary lesbian fiction

P.O. Box 10543, Tallahassee, FL 32302
Phone: 800-729-4992
www.bellabooks.com

WITHOUT WARNING: Book one in the Shaken series by KG MacGregor. *Without Warning* is the story of their courageous journey through adversity, and their promise of steadfast love.
ISBN: 978-1-59493-120-8
$13.95

THE CANDIDATE by Tracey Richardson. Presidential candidate Jane Kincaid had always expected the road to the White House would exact a high personal toll. She just never knew how high until forced to choose between her heart and her political destiny.
ISBN: 978-1-59493-133-8
$13.95

TALL IN THE SADDLE by Karin Kallmaker, Barbara Johnson, Therese Szymanski and Julia Watts. The playful quartet that penned the acclaimed *Once Upon A Dyke* and *Stake Through the Heart* are back and now turning to the Wild (and Very Hot) West to bring you another collection of erotically charged, action-packed tales.
ISBN: 978-1-59493-106-2
$15.95

IN THE NAME OF THE FATHER by Gerri Hill. In this highly anticipated sequel to *Hunter's Way*, Dallas Homicide Detectives Tori Hunter and Samantha Kennedy investigate the murder of a Catholic priest who is found naked and strangled to death.
ISBN: 978-1-59493-108-6
$13.95